A heartbeat after he hu from his perch atop the green brilliance, Zorro lit in a different direction. H .... toward the ground, its fuse sizzling, then shielded his eyes as a glaring scarlet fireball erupted to the right of the jail-house, flinging off showery mountains of sparks.

He held his improvised lighter to another grenade, wound up for a throw as its fuse hissed down to a spar-kling nub, pitched it over the opposite side of the roof, and then tossed the remaining fireworks in rapid suc-cession, turning the plaza into a demon bowl of vari-colored flame. The night throbbed and swirled with bangs and flashes. Streaks of violet scribbled the dark-ness. Brimstone yellow clouds floated in the air like glow-ing, smoky wraiths. Pink, blue, and white pinwheels zipped past each other in crazily looping trajectories. Rose-red blossoms expanded with convulsive force, hung briefly above the plaza, and then dispersed, breaking apart into scattered, shimmering petals.

Zorro had barely released his final grenade when the jailhouse door slammed open and nearly a half dozen men came rushing out into the plaza, all of them wear-ing the blue uniforms and crossbands of King's lancers, all shouting in bewilderment, and all about to have the biggest surprise of the night literally drop down on their heads.

JEROME PREISLER

ZORRO

AND THE
JAGUAR WARRIORS

A TOM DOHERTY ASSOCIATES BOOK
NEW YORK

This is a work of fiction. All the characters and events portrayed in this book are either products of the author's imagination or are used fictitiously.

ZORRO AND THE JAGUAR WARRIORS

Copyright © 1998 by Zorro Productions, Inc.

A Forge Book
Published by Tom Doherty Associates, Inc.
175 Fifth Avenue
New York, NY 10010

Forge® is a registered trademark of Tom Doherty Associates, Inc.

ISBN: 0-812-56767-6

First edition: September 1998

Printed in the United States of America

0 9 8 7 6 5 4 3 2 1

We would like to thank Ric Meyers—author, action expert, and pop culture authority extraordinaire—for his invaluable assistance in completing this adventure.

Chapter 1

The four of them slipped between the shadows crowding the moonlit plaza, passing stalls still hung with flowers and banners after the long holiday festivities. Their movement did nothing to disturb the silence, complete now except for stray bursts of laughter from the cantina, where men were doing their best to sustain the high spirit of the carnival with swigs of wine and *pulque*, dice games, and jests sprinkled with language they never would have repeated in the company of their wives and daughters.

Crouched beneath a makeshift awning at the opposite corner of the plaza, Arcadia Flores held out her lantern and peered into the merchant booth where, just hours ago, she had displayed her handwoven blankets, *serapes*, and *rebozos* for potential buyers. Behind her, the pair of scrawny, crop-eared mules hitched to her cart were pawing the ground with their hooves, as if indicating their impatience to head home for the night.

Well, Arcadia thought, they were no more anxious than she was to get underway, and would simply have to bear with her a short while longer. Traveling in the dark was nothing she would have ordinarily chosen to do—in fact, it was only after she'd been well out on the trail climbing toward her family's adobe that she realized what she had left behind, and had doubled back toward the pueblo in the hope of finding it in the stall.

She frowned. How could she have been so careless as to lose the brooch? Hundreds of people had thronged the plaza that afternoon, elegant señoras and ranchos from the big haciendas noisily jostling up against servants, farm workers, *aguadores,* rodeo horsemen, ragtag peasant children, beggars with dirty outstretched palms, missionary padres in shovel hats, jugglers, magicians, minstrels, soldiers, politicians, Indians, other peddlers. Anyone might have chanced to find it after she'd left. And what if it had fallen off elsewhere? After all, she had no recollection of the clasp coming open. It could have happened at any time of the day . . . when she was loading her unsold goods back onto the cart, or before that, when she had been drawn to one of the cooking pits by the delicious aroma of spiced beef roasting over live oak coals.

At any time.

Arcadia shuffled further into the empty stall, the hem of her muslin skirt bunched around her ankles, her free hand feeling for the pin on the dusty earth. While hardly valuable, it was well-crafted and made of pure silver. No doubt it would bring a fair number of pesos to anyone who traded it in at one of the local shops, or sold it to some dashing young *caballero* out to gain the favor of a woman in these celebratory days of carnival and Lent.

She would never forgive herself if . . .

Arcadia's frown lengthened. The burros had become more agitated, whinnying, stamping the ground in nervous little jumps. What was wrong with them? She looked uneasily behind her, bringing her lamp around from under the awning, adding its illumination to the pale light of the moon.

A startled breath hissed out through her front teeth.

Less than three feet away, the huge grey face of a rat was staring down at her from atop the body of a man.

"Hello, señorita. If I'd known such wares as yours could be found in these filthy stalls, I would have visited them sooner."

There was a dry chuckle from the shadows behind the rat-faced man.

Arcadia shifted her gaze toward the sound of the laughter, and felt the skin crawl on her neck and arms. The terrifying figure had three companions . . . all of them similarly grotesque. To its left stood the walking image of Death, tall and draped in long black robes, a scythe clenched in its hand, a battered straw sombrero balanced almost ludicrously on its grinning, fleshless skull. On the other side was man bundled in the rotting blankets and torn leather breeches of a leper, wearing a scapulary medallion around his neck, straggles of filthy hair spilling out from under the folds of a tattered gray hood. A dagger gleamed in his fist like a metal fang.

Standing beside him, the fourth member of the bizarre group bore a sword in one hand and a scale in the other, looking for all the world like Saint Michael the Archangel . . . armed for battle against Satan, and charged with weighing souls for ascension to heaven or banishment to hell.

Conscious of her heart beating rapidly in her chest, Arcadia tried to calm herself with a deep breath. The three days preceding Ash Wednesday were occasions for a great many pageants and masquerades throughout the pueblo, and it was not unusual to see men dressed up in elaborate costumes, playing practical jokes, teasing women, sometimes acting like wild, boisterous children . . . especially after they had lingered in the cantina too long. Although Arcadia did not view herself as the striking beauty others saw her to be, she nevertheless recognized that she was young and attractive, and had expected she would have to tolerate her share of foolish pranks. But it did not seem to her that these men were merely being nuisances.

These men, the way they laughed, the way they were pressing in on her . . .

She rose to her feet and slowly backed away from them, trying to settle the mules with gentle strokes of her hand.

These men radiated menace.

"Don't worry about the beasts," Death's Head said. He tapped the point of his scythe with his fingertip. "The four of us are in much greater need of your attention."

The man in the leper suit cackled. It was a sound like dry chips of stone grating together.

"A woman's touch to soothe the agonized flesh," he said. "A kiss to lift the curse from my body."

Arcadia withdrew another step.

"Leave me alone," she said. "You've all had too much to drink and are asking for trouble . . ."

The Rat Man shook his head. "We do not *ask* for anything, my pretty señorita," he said. "What we want, we take."

"Please, I have nothing for you . . ."

"Ah, but here you are wrong again," the Rat Man said.

His voice muffled by the mask.

Staring at her . . .

Staring through the small round eyeholes of the mask.

"There are the profits you brought in for the rags you were selling today," he said. "And there are other things you can offer that will keep us satisfied for a good long while."

She kept backing away. Her fingers fluttered to her shawl and pulled its flaps more tightly together.

"Don't do this," she said. "The men in the cantina . . . the soldiers in there . . . they'll hear . . ."

Death's Head shot his arm out, grabbed her hand, and tore it away from her neck with a jerk that made her groan in pain. As she struggled to free herself from his grip, he hooked one side of her shawl onto his scythe, pulling it open until it slipped off her shoulders and fell to the ground like a shed skin.

"Cry out, *mi canaria,*" he said, twisting her wrist, sliding the cold, curved edge of the scythe across her throat, "and it'll be the last song you sing in this lifetime."

"I think you have nothing to fear from rattling bones and squealing rodents, señorita," a man's voice abruptly said from somewhere to Arcadia's right. "For they are far uglier than dangerous, and make only senseless, idiotic noises."

The blade froze against Arcadia's neck. Death's Head glanced distractedly into the heavy shadows, searching for the newcomer, swiveling his upper body to compensate for the limits his mask put on his peripheral vision.

Keeping her own head very still under the scythe, Arcadia also flicked her eyes in the direction of the voice.

There was nothing to be seen. Nothing but the front of the blacksmith's shop, its entrance dark and vacant, the baked clay tiles above the portico looking faintly silver in a wash of moonlight

"Where's the coward who shoots off his mouth, then hides from us?" Death's Head grunted.

The mules heaved and shuffled. Otherwise, the silence was complete.

The Archangel looked tensely from side to side. "Show yourself!"

More silence.

Death's Head turned his attention back to Arcadia. "Your friend seems to have thought twice about the cost of heroism, pretty one. But perhaps we should bring you to a place where there'll be no further chance of interrup—"

For Arcadia, everything that followed seemed to happen in the space of a single moment. There was a loud echoing *crack!* accompanied by a rush of wind against her face, and then Death's Head emitted a shrill yelp of pain, his hand leaping backward, away from her neck, the scythe flying from his fingers and dropping harmlessly to the ground. His heels scuffed on the dirt as he whirled around in a jerky half circle, making Arcadia think of a fish wriggling at the end of a line . . .

"*Ay*, let me go!" Death's Head mewled. Coiled like a smooth black snake, whatever was wrapped around his wrist had shredded his jacket sleeve and bitten deeply into his flesh.

His eyes bulging under his mask, he tried to claw himself free, and had no sooner registered that he'd been snagged by the tapered end of a bullwhip before a powerful tug of the lash hauled him off his feet.

"How easily the Reaper is conquered," his unseen attacker said as he fell to his hands and knees. "Let him see what it is to lay among the dust and worms like those whose lives he would take."

Death's Head thrashed on the ground, whimpering, blood ribboning from his arm. Rat Man, the Archangel and the Leper were all snapping their heads back and forth, peering into the opaque shadows.

"*Quièn esta?*" the leper rasped. "Who are you?"

Rooted in place, her brown eyes wide with amazement, Arcadia already knew the answer.

Standing several feet in front of her was a lean figure in black, his gloved hand gripping the handle of the whip, a highwayman's mask concealing his face beneath a broad-brimmed sombrero. A cape flowed from his shoulders like a strip cut out of the night, its folds partially covering the ornate silver sword hilt against his hip.

"El Zorro," Arcadia muttered breathlessly. "The Fox."

For months she had been hearing rumors of a masked man who tore through the night like a fury, a champion of justice for the common citizens of *El Pueblo de Los Angeles*, a recurring horror to their oppressors. But she had believed him a legend, a symbol of the people's hope and desire rather than an existing being . . . spirit, human, or otherwise.

She sucked in a breath. The Archangel was coming directly toward Zorro from behind, his sword raised for a lethal strike.

Arcadia started to mouth a warning, but before she could find her voice, Zorro flicked back his wrist and his bullwhip unwound from Death Head's arm like a living thing. It went whistling back over his shoulder, its tip striking the ground in front of the Archangel with a crisp snap, halting him in his tracks.

It was, Arcadia thought incredulously, as if Zorro had somehow *felt* him approaching . . . as if he possessed the sharper-than-human senses of his namesake.

Now he spun around on his bootheels and faced the man in the angel costume.

"I would recommend you take flight while you can, but it seems you've been stripped of your wings," he said, a smile flashing across his lips. "Fallen from grace, I suppose."

The Archangel kept his sword at the ready.

"You won't be so so quick with your tongue after you've tasted steel, *cabrón*," he said, and lunged forward.

Zorro dropped his right hand to his side and drew his own sword. Its polished blade threw off bright slivers of moonlight as it streaked from its scabbard.

The Archangel stabbed out with his weapon, putting his entire body behind the thrust, but the black-clad avenger nimbly moved back and swept his blade up and sideways, crossing it with his attacker's, deflecting the sword point from his chest. The Archangel stumbled a moment, his shoulder wrenched by the force of the parry. Then he released an inarticulate growl of frustration and came at Zorro a second time, his right hand bringing the sword down toward his throat, his other hand gripping the scale by the middle as if it were a truncheon. Its pans clattered noisily at either end.

In the instant it took him to react, Zorro noticed Rat Man running toward him from his right, and quickly saw how he might stop both attackers at once. He would need precision and timing . . . and most of all surprise.

As the Archangel plunged closer, Zorro shifted slightly to his left, grasped the arm which held the club, and then leveraged it to the right. The club smashed into Rat Man's head before the Archangel could think to drop it, striking with an audible *crunch*. At the same time, Zorro brought his right knee up into the Archangel's groin and he doubled over in agony, gasping, the muscles of his face bulging and contorted.

The two men teetered in separate directions, the Archangel dropping his weapons and clutching himself with both hands, Rat Man releasing a groan through his shattered mask before falling over on his back.

Zorro stepped in front of the Archangel, kicking his sword and makeshift club out of reach before he could grab for them. Then he wheeled toward the spot where he'd last seen the fourth member of the group.

The Leper stood several feet away with his arm held straight out in front of him, a pistol in his clenched fist. Zorro caught a brief but clear glimpse of it in the moonlight and immediately identified it as a double-barreled English flintlock. Each barrel had a separate lock and would afford one shot before the gunman had to reload.

Zorro inhaled. Most of the shortarms he'd seen in the New World were of the single-barrel, one-shot design. But the Englishmen were fond of seeking ways to improve their rate of fire, and had even experimented with revolving cylinders that would contain as many as five or six loads. It was only a matter of time before the innovations were perfected and these multiple-shot weapons began to proliferate.

He did not like guns. Guns made killing easy, and so depreciated life.

Did not like them, especially when they were aimed at him.

Using his cloak almost as a magician would when creating a distraction, Zorro swept it around his body in a wide fan. The ploy had its desired effect. There was a sudden crash as the trigger was squeezed and the upper gunbarrel spat out its charge, sending the ball-shaped projectile well to the left of Zorro amid a shower of sparks.

He rearranged his cape again, then tucked his chin low to his chest and dove to the ground, launching himself toward his enemy with an acrobatic forward roll. The Leper lowered his weapon's muzzle and blasted out a second shot, but Zorro had already changed direction and gone tumbling sideways into the darkness, vanishing from sight in the space between seconds.

The Leper's eyes darted one way, then another, his breaths coming in rapid, excited snatches.

"Any fool can shoot one of those things . . . but hitting your target is another matter," Zorro said, standing behind the Leper now, perfectly still, throwing his voice so it seemed to come floating from across the plaza—another trick he'd borrowed from those practiced in the conjuring arts.

The Leper pivoted toward where he thought Zorro might be. He was not a superstitious man, but the way the voice had drifted out of nowhere, whispery and disembodied . . . it had frightened him, frightened him badly. Perhaps this Zorro was indeed the raging spirit the *peónes* claimed he was.

He reached nervously for a leather ammunition pack beneath his robes, his hand fumbling its flap open. Trembling, slick with sweat, his other hand gripped the exhausted weapon.

His heart pounding in his chest, he craned his head further into the darkness.

"Where have you gone, you slinking dog?" he said.

There was no response.

At the far end of the plaza he heard a door slam open. Then the overlapping voices of men came brewing from the cantina.

The gunshots, he thought.

They must have heard the gunshots, been drawn outside by the gunshots.

He considered taking to his heels, but then imagined Zorro hovering out in the night somewhere, imagined blindly running into him, and concentrated on getting fresh loads out of the pack without having them slip from his jittery fingers. His fear was unbearable now, eating away at him like some toothy internal parasite.

Zorro, meanwhile, had moved closer to him, silently drawing his sword again, his eyes narrowing with interest as he noted the loads the gunner had extracted from under his garments. Rather than carry the ball ammunition, gunpowder, and wadding material in separate pouches, he was using combustible linen cartridges of the sort devised by—and supplied to—the military.

"Very well, then," the Leper said, steadying his hand enough to feed a cartridge into each barrel. "Hide from me all you want. The woman is dead."

He jerked his gun toward Arcadia, who had remained near her burro cart, immobilized with terror.

She stared at his pistol, her eyes stunned and glassy. Her gasping intake of breath was all there was to show she understood what was happening.

The Leper cocked the dual hammers of his pistol, tightened his finger over the trigger . . . and suddenly felt something sharp press into the back of his neck.

"Pass me your weapon this instant, my poor *lépero*, or I will greatly hasten the progress of your affliction with my sword," Zorro said from behind him, his voice a scarcely more than a whisper.

The Leper froze. He licked his lips, hesitating uncertainly.

"The pistol," Zorro said, his gloved hand reaching around the gunner's side. He jabbed the soft flesh below his ear with the sword point. "Now."

The Leper winced, a trickle of blood running down his neck.

"Go ahead," he said shakily. His fist loosened around the gun butt. "Take it."

Zorro snatched the pistol from his fingers and slipped it into his belt. He had to finish his work quickly now. To judge by the racket they were making, the men from the cantina were very close, and he was certain there would be soldiers among them

. . . none of whom were apt to be admirers, given the Governor's labeling of him as a wanted outlaw.

He grasped the Leper's shoulder, spun him around so they were facing each other, and swept back his hood with a deft flick of his sword.

The thick, gimlet-eyed face of the man looking fearfully back at Zorro brought a smile of secret amusement to his face.

He tossed a glance over his shoulder, his roguish grin expanding. Lumbering toward him at the front of the crowd was Sergeant Garcia himself, his enormous gut doubtless sloshing with wine.

"*Madre de dios!*" Garcia shouted to the men at his rear. His eyes were bloodshot above his pouchy, unshaven cheeks. "It is the fox!"

Without wasting a moment, Zorro slashed his sword across the cowering robber's chest—once across to the left, diagonally downward to the right, then straight back to the left.

Etching the sign of the "Z" on his ragged garments.

"Garcia, how nice to see you are enjoying the *fiesta!*" he shouted, and spun toward the approaching crowd again. "Before I run off, let me wish you peace and good will . . . and if you don't mind, suggest that your troops find better ways to occupy themselves than harassing innocent women. It appears these robbing scoundrels are, in fact, soldiers from your *cuartel.*"

"Choke on your advice *and* your good wishes!" Garcia slurred, staggering forward. He reached for his sword, but drunkenly misjudged where its hilt would be, his hand overshooting it by several inches and closing around empty air. "The only scoundrel I see is you, and once I pull my blade you'll be sorry—"

He blinked, frowned down at the sword handle as if it had jumped to elude his grasp, and grabbed for it again . . . but the sudden movement upset his precarious balance and he crashed onto his bottom, his legs sprawled out in a wide V.

No less soused than Garcia, the men behind him exploded with laughter.

Zorro decided to take his leave while they were still feeling mirthful . . . and before they remembered the huge reward out on his head.

His cloak flapping behind him, he turned and raced over to Arcadia.

"*Buenos noches,* señorita," he said, doffing his hat. "Are you feeling all right?"

She looked at him a moment. Her expression remained confused, but some of the shock had drained out of it.

"Yes." She nodded slowly. "Thank you."

Zorro smiled, bent to pick up her shawl, slapped the dust off it, and gently covered her shoulders. "Rest assured, your trip home will be safe from this point on . . . for though you may not see me, I will be watching over you the entire way."

He bowed extravagantly and then turned for a parting glance at the sergeant and his drinking companions. Four of Garcia's men were struggling to haul him back onto his feet—two with their hands under his right arm, the other two pulling up on his left side—but as far as Zorro could see they were having little success.

"*Uno, dos, tres . . . ahora!*" Garcia shouted, signaling the group to heave.

They did so all at once, grunting and sighing with effort, managing to get Garcia partway off the ground before two of them buckled under the strain, their legs loosely giving out, flopping over him in a tangled heap.

Zorro threw back his head, produced a throaty, roguish laugh, and then dashed off into the shadows hemming the plaza.

Seconds later, he was gone.

 *Chapter 2*

Don Alejandro de la Vega's sprawling hacienda occupied 30,000 acres of prime cattle land atop a bluff overlooking the Pacific Ocean, with the Santa Monica mountains to the north and the San Gabriels bumping up against the sky to the southeast. The dry climate and high elevation made spectacular views of the surrounding landscape possible by day, and allowed for equally crystalline perspectives of the heavens after sundown—a fact which enchanted Alejandro's son Diego to no end. Gazing up at the bright, scattered stars had been one of his favorite pastimes since boyhood, offering a tranquil solitude, a sort of lonely but inviting freedom that would always rouse visions of soaring above the world without fear or inhibition, dark wings spread against the jeweled black sky, sailing higher and higher, like some wild nocturnal creature whose eyes missed nothing that happened below.

Impressed by his son's intellect and unbounded curiosity, Don Alejandro had sent him off to be schooled at the University of Madrid when he was seventeen. There Diego disciplined his mind with studies ranging from mathematics to science to the fine arts, nourished his spirit with the philosophies and mystical teachings of faraway lands, and honed his body and reflexes learning how to fence from a master swordsman. While in the Spanish capital, he had also developed an eye for beautiful women, and been known to pursue them with a romantic vigor surpassed only by his appetite for knowledge.

Proud as he was of Diego's academic accomplishments, Alejandro had been privately disappointed by his failure to apply his extraordinary mind and skills to productive endeavors. The blunt truth was that he had been something of an idler ever since returning to California upon completion of his education. He typically slept late into the morning. He had no interest in participating in the operation of the ranch, or for that matter entering into any other profitable trade. Though charming and well-mannered, he had few close personal relationships and was distracted much of the time, escaping into daydreams whenever he had the chance, spending hours staring out at the sea or wandering the fields near the hacienda. He resisted speaking of political events within the Empire and its settlements, preferring to turn conversations toward some new scientific theory, musical composition, or favorite book. As far as Alejandro could tell, the only thing that ever pulled his head out of the clouds was the smile of a pretty señorita . . . in that respect, at least, Diego retained the energy and focus that had characterized his years as a student.

Diego's failure to measure up to his early promise had brought about tensions between father and son that had yet to be openly acknowledged by either, but could be felt by anyone visiting their home. Having lost his beloved wife Rosa to disease when Diego was an adolescent, Alejandro sometimes wondered whether he had met his responsibilities as the young man's remaining parent . . . and in his secret heart believed that he hadn't. Furthermore, he himself had been suffering from ill health in recent months, and was concerned that Diego would be unprepared to lead a successful life if anything happened to him.

These worries were very much at the front of his mind as Diego entered the salon this morning, dressed in a brocaded silk robe, his shock of glossy dark hair mussed from sleep, his blue eyes somewhat puffed, looking as if he'd left a large part of himself behind in bed.

"Ah, father, if I'd known we were having company I would have greeted the day sooner," he said, and tipped a gracious bow to the fellow on the sofa across the room, recognizing him vaguely as one of the pueblo's substantial landholders.

Alejandro looked at him over a steaming teacup, not quite frowning. A thin, aristocratic man of fifty with snow-white hair and an elegantly trimmed beard, he was seated near the window in his favorite armchair, a high-backed Louis XIV he'd imported from France along with the rest of the salon furnishings—the single exception being a mahogany and satinwood piano Diego had ordered from the influential workshop of Duncan Phyfe, while on a trip to the *Yanqui* city of New York.

Diego approached the guest, his hand extended. "Good morning, Señor . . ."

"Don Pedro Morales, this is my son Diego," Alejandro said, willing the scowl off his forehead, hoping he hadn't betrayed his embarrassment over his son's late rising . . . and seeming unfamiliarity with a man of great distinction. "Don Morales produces the best citrus crop in California some miles west of here, in San Fernando."

"Ah yes. The valley is a green paradise," Diego said. He yawned and smoothed his pencil-thin mustache. "I once attended a *fandango* at the estate of an orange grower there named Vasquez. At the invitation of the lovely belle of the house."

"I know the family well." Morales smiled. "As for the land, I would indeed be a fool to complain about it. The groves are bountiful, and the climate reminds me much of my native Valencia."

Diego thought he sensed an undertone of hesitation in his voice.

"And yet . . . ?" he prompted.

Morales's expression seemed both surprised and a bit uncomfortable.

"You are very perceptive, Diego," he said, and adjusted a pair of spectacles on his long, hawkish nose. "Perhaps it is the isolation or the difficulty of transporting provisions over the mountains. But I sometimes miss living in more populated territory."

"That is quite understandable," Diego said, yawning again. "I must admit to enjoying the vitality of the pueblo, which is the closest thing we in the borderlands have to a true city. The gaiety that filled the plaza this past week was exhilarating, and I couldn't help but throw myself into it . . . as you may have surmised from my worn appearance."

"To be truthful, I'd wondered how a young man of such obvious good health could awaken looking so, ah, unrefreshed," Morales said, lifting his own teacup from the table in front of him. "Did you attend the masquerade ball last night?"

"For a time, yes. Although, as far as my social pleasures go, I prefer to stay on the move, making each moment a new adventure," Diego said with a wry smile.

Alejandro glanced at his son from an oval of sunlight pouring through the casement window.

"Odd," he said. "I hadn't seen you preparing a costume."

"That is because I went as myself, Father," Diego said, still smiling. "Why wear a disguise, when I am already a notorious prowler of the night?"

"At least when it comes to the ladies, I've heard," Morales said.

He and Diego both laughed.

Alejandro watched them quietly, eager to change the subject. Bad enough his son had come dragging in from his bedroom barely half an hour before noon, he did not want him going into detail about his social pleasures, as Diego had put it. You never knew whose daughter had been involved, and the last thing he needed was a scandal involving his only heir.

"Why don't you have a cup of tea and join us, Diego?" he said. "Don Morales was just telling me of a troubling situation in the countryside beyond his lands."

"And among the Indians and peasant workers who

tend my farm," Morales added. "It seemed to me that, as a member of the town council, your father should be informed."

"Oh?" Diego leaned over the table, reached for the teapot, and tilted its spout over an empty cup. "I wasn't aware there'd been problems."

"There haven't, exactly," Morales said, and shrugged a little. "But as they say in Mexico, the person who does not look ahead stays behind."

Diego sat in the chair across from Morales and drank his tea. It was a native variety that tasted mildly of berries. The patch of sunshine around Alejandro had been absorbed into a flood of midday light from the veranda that brightened and warmed the room, and sparkled off the delicate porcelain handle of Diego's cup.

"You're sounding very mysterious," he said.

"Then I apologize, for it isn't my intention." Morales straightened in his seat. "It's just that I can't quite put my finger on what is going on at *Los Rayos del Sol.*"

"Now I'm truly confused." Diego looked at him thoughtfully. "Isn't that a backcountry mission that's been helping out the poor?"

"Yes and no," Morales said. "Certainly it is in a remote location. And you are correct that its founders have been dispensing food, clothing, and even medical treatment to those in need. But in the sense that it is sanctioned by neither the Spanish government, nor a link in the chain of Franciscan outposts along the *camino real* . . . well, I have some difficulty calling it a true mission."

Diego shrugged. "You will forgive me for saying so, but many wrongs are committed under the guise of

Christian piety, and the Cross is too often a symbol of power and conquest rather than tolerance. If my travels have taught me anything, it is that there are many different paths between body and soul. Each man should be allowed to choose for himself which to take—or whether to take any at all."

"As you know, son, I share your belief that it is wrong to impose our religious faith upon others," Alejandro said. "However, there are disturbing circumstances in this instance that have nothing to do with a clash between cultures." He sighed and glanced at Morales. "Perhaps you should tell him about the night walkers."

Diego looked puzzled. "Night walkers? I don't understand."

Morales brought his cup away from his mouth and watched him through rising curls of steam.

"Let me start at the beginning," he said very slowly. "Perhaps six months ago, soon after I received word that an area some miles from my lands was being cleared and irrigated by *Indios,* I rode out with several hands to investigate. What we found were anything but proper dwellings—that is, crude thatched huts contained within a perimeter of wooden posts that had been driven into the ground at wide intervals. There were perhaps thirty men and women . . . neither Yang Na, Mariposa, Chumash, nor members any other tribe I could identify. Their language was also foreign to me. But they didn't appear hostile, and while I'm hardly as enlightened you or your father, I decided to let them be. As long as their little community wasn't causing problems, their arrival seemed none of my affair." He paused, extracted something from his jacket pocket, and laid it down on the table in front of him. "They gave us quite a few gifts before we turned back to my hacienda . . . and this is one of them."

Diego reached for the object and examined it with interest. A medicine pouch resembling those worn by many local Indian tribes, it was unusual only in the sort of animal skin it was made of.

"This looks like the pelt of a spotted cat," he said, turning the pouch in his hands. It was a tawny color, with black rosette-shaped markings. "A jaguar, if I were to guess."

Morales nodded, regarding him through his lenses.

"A few of the men at the settlement had cloaks of this jaguar-skin covering their whole bodies, along with mantles that were actually fashioned from the heads of the beasts," he said. "My impression was that they were of a ruling class. Priests or chieftains."

"And the rest? How did they dress?"

"In the loincloths of common workers . . . each with a paw of the same animal hanging from it."

Diego continued to study the pouch, pressing his fingers into it. The sleepiness had left his features.

"May I have a look at its contents?" he asked.

Morales threw out his hand in a gesture for him to go ahead.

Diego carefully pulled open the pouch's leather drawstring and turned it upside down over his palm. A small quantity of leafy bundles came spilling out. He examined them for a moment, then lifted his hand to his nose and sniffed them curiously. The scent wafting off them was musky and resinous.

"The leaf packets are filled with some kind of fermented substance, probably a pulped root," he said, returning them to the pouch. "As someone who has studied the use of plants as remedies, I find this interesting. It also intrigues me that the garments and fetishes you described aren't like any clan emblems I've seen in California. But, if I may be direct, Don Morales, you said that your only concern was whether the *Indios* presented a threat . . . which they didn't. Why are these things important to you? And what is the connection between the Indians and these night walkers you mentioned? And of either to *Los Rayos del Sol*?"

Morales inhaled, then released his breath in a sigh. From outside came the raucous chattering of magpies.

"After my introduction to the Indian camp I didn't return there for a long time. Forgot about it, really. Then, much later, I began to hear about this place, *Los Rayos del Sol*. The peasants would occasionally speak of going there for charitable meals of mutton stew and *frijoles*, free clothing, that sort of thing. I had no specific idea where it was and, again, didn't make it my concern. There are the daily matters that occupy our minds, you understand.

"Then, last month, three of my best laborers disappeared. These were brothers from the Yang Na village who shared a lodging on my hacienda. At first, no one was concerned. Sometimes when the men get a little money in their pockets, they head into the pueblo to gamble and drink. Sometimes they meet women and you don't hear from them for a few days. You know how it goes. The whisky and pesos run out and they return to work. These three never did, though. I organized a search, sent people to ask around after them. But they learned nothing. No one had seen them. No one had any idea where they might be. It was as if they had been swept off the earth." Morales paused. He had put down his tea. His hands clasped tightly together on his lap. "A week later another worker vanished without a trace. Then, four days later, a *mestizo* named Paulo. He was with me for over fifteen years. His wife is a cook in my household. I have paid for his boys to attend school and get books to read. Paulo was a loyal and responsible man who delighted in his wife and children. Yet one day he went out to till the fields and wasn't seen again . . . until five days ago. Fully three weeks later."

He was quiet again. Diego observed that he was wringing his hands but made no comment, giving him a chance to organize his thoughts.

"I'd sent a couple of hands up to the pueblo for some feed and other items the day before. They'd slept overnight at an inn, and were on their way back to the hacienda with a wagonload of supplies when they saw Paulo wandering aimlessly along the side of the road, his eyes staring straight ahead like those of someone in a trance. His appearance had so changed they were almost unable to recognize him. He had no recollection at all of where he'd been. He barely seemed to know his own name. He was unshaven and disheveled and had lost a tremendous amount of weight. And he had a pouch exactly like the one I just showed you hanging from a lanyard around his neck."

Diego's brows arched under his mass of dark hair. He leaned forward, eyes intent on Morales.

"Has his memory since returned?" he asked.

"Of almost everything except the period of his absence. That is a blank to him."

"How is he otherwise?"

Morales shook his head sadly. "Paulo isn't the man that he was. He is perhaps forty years old, and had been very able-bodied. Now seems like someone of sixty. His mind has lost its sharpness. His dedication to work and family is gone. I do not believe in witches . . . but I swear to you both, it is as if a spell has been put on him."

Diego thought a moment.

"You've told me you didn't go back to the Indian camp for a while after your first visit, which suggests that you did return there at some point," he said.

"Don Morales went on out to the settlement yesterday afternoon," Alejandro said, breaking his silence. "He was about to tell me what he learned when you entered the parlor."

Both Diego and his father looked at Morales.

The landholder twisted his hands.

"I left the hacienda with the same team of riders who'd been with me previously. On our last trip, the trail leading to side of the valley where the Indians had struck camp could hardly be negotiated through the chaparral. Now it had been widened, leveled and cleared of overgrowth. An astounding thing. We didn't understand it. And then came much more we were unable to understand." He took another deep breath, in through the mouth, out through the nose. "As we came within a mile or so of the camp, we began to encounter men and women traveling in the same direction on foot. They were pulling carts loaded with hay, earth and rocks along the roadway, some walking alone, some in scattered groups. I recognized a few of them from the crews of other *hacendados*. All were peasants or Indians. All were in the same dazed state Paulo had been in when he was found by my men. And all wore leopard-skin pouches around their necks."

"*Fuego de dios,*" Alejandro said. "I've heard nothing stranger in my entire life."

"Nor I," Diego said.

"Hear the end of my story before you make that judgement, my friends," Morales said. He nibbled on his lower lip. His meshed knuckles were white. "With these people on every side of us, we made our way up toward the Indian camp . . . but had only gotten to its outer perimeter when we beheld something that compelled us to reign in our horses. We stayed there a moment and went no further. A half dozen grown men, men who fancy ourselves as rugged, yet we were as frightened as babes." He chewed his lip some more. "Like the trail, the settlement had grown tremendously and now sprawled across an area four or five times larger than it had occupied months before. The straw-roofed huts remained only at its edges. And in the center of the camp was some sort of temple. A pyramid. Not yet complete, but already towering perhaps fifty feet in the air. I cannot tell you what it is to come upon such a sight. Even from a distance, we could see some of the carvings on the outside wall. They were of jaguars. Marching jaguars. And there was something else carved into the stone. An inscription near the highest part of the pyramid . . . written in Spanish."

Diego was still sitting forward in his chair, concentrating on his every word.

"The writing . . . what did it say?"

Morales eyes flicked down to his knuckes, then over to Alejandro, then back on Diego.

"*Los Rayos del Sol,*" he said. "Without looking for it, I had located the mission."

Chapter 3

Lost in contemplation, Diego wound his way around a broad shoulder of rock, his feet clinging to the twisting path, easily moving down the hillside. The sun shone hotly on his neck and shoulders, but the dry air evaporated his sweat as fast as it left his pores. There was a prismatic quality to the light, a salt tang in the breeze, that hinted of nearness to the sea. Rooted in the dun-colored sandstone, huge, columnar Joshua trees stood with their branches elbowing skyward as if in fervent worship.

Now Diego paused to listen, a smile touching his lips. Although thickets of *ocatillo* and scrub oak screened the valley below from sight, he could hear the smooth, rolling rhythm of hoofbeats in the updrafts common at this time of day.

Tornado was out running. Getting his exercise. The confidence and exhilaration of the stallion's stride was unmistakable. Like the sound of a great heart racing with joy.

Diego resumed walking, Don Morales's jaguar-skin pouch in hand, the bright openness of his surroundings helping him to feel completely alert for the first time since he'd awakened. A short while ago he had excused himself from the parlor, then washed, dressed, eaten a quick breakfast, and started out down the slope. He had been anxious to share Morales's baffling story with Bernardo, show him the pouch, and see whether he might have any helpful thoughts.

You never knew with him. Bernardo was not merely unpredictable, he took enormous pleasure from surprising people, especially those to whom he felt closest. Often he would give you a look that was so obtuse, you had to wonder if he was deaf as well as mute . . . as everyone but Diego had been fooled into believing was the case. At other times, however, he would flash on some brilliant insight, his hands and fingers signing almost too rapidly for the eye to follow, as if he were afraid it might flee his mind uncommunicated. That mind, with all its complicated processes and eccentricities, had always been a fascinating puzzle to Diego. He was convinced he would never entirely understand it, a realization which might have prompted some men to give up trying. Yet somehow it only stoked his interest.

About ten or fifteen yards from the spot where he'd first heard Tornado's thundering hooves, Diego swung off the narrow path and continued climbing downward over brambles and rocky debris. He moved no less steadily over the talus than he had higher up the slope, having taken this route more times than he possibly could have counted since discovering the cave entrance . . . *how* long ago had it been? Hard to believe over ten years had passed. A decade and spare change since a boy with more curiosity than good sense had gone straying from his parents' supervision, and chanced to discover a cave that would become the hidden lair of *El Zorro*.

Now he reached the bottom of the canyon and circled the hill to a niche in its eastern slope. Thorny brush and boulders rising high to his left and right, Diego moved into the shadow of an overhang that blocked any view of him from above. Then he sought out a barely visible hummock and stepped on it with all his weight, depressing a square metal plate buried in the dirt underfoot.

An instant later, a gaping hole seemed to appear in the rugged face of the hill. In fact, an artfully camouflaged door, indistinguishable from the surrounding rock when closed, had swung open on a concealed system of weights, rods, and pulleys that had been activated by the lowered pressure plate.

Striding past the mouth of the cave, Diego reached overhead, tugged down on a dangling coil of rope, and was immediately thrown into gloom as the door swiveled shut behind him, once again merging with the hillside.

He advanced through the subterranean corridor, moving downward along a gentle grade, his way illuminated by kerosene lamps hung from spikes in its bare stone walls. He heard a flinty, rhythmic grinding sound up ahead and smiled a little, recognizing it as that of metal scraping against stone.

A short distance beyond its entrance, the passage began to widen out on either side. The sound was closer. Diego walked a little further, turned a bend, and emerged onto a shallow ledge projecting above an immense, vaulted chamber. The pale orange glow of the lanterns flung crisscrossing shadows over the grooves and folds of its limestone walls. Bats flapped and churned between stalactites in its lofty heights. All around him, moisture glistened on delicate, spidery crystal formations shaped by centuries of dripping water.

The grinding noise was very loud now, coming from across the cavernous space.

Some men never rested, treating each moment as if it were a hole that needed filling, Diego thought.

He looked down and felt a swell of affection.

There below him in a sort of natural alcove, Bernardo sat hunched over a sharpening wheel, his feet working its pedals, his back to the ledge on which Diego stood watching him. Sparks of light flew off into the dimness from the long shiny blade in his hand. He seemed oblivious to his visitor's arrival.

Diego stepped off the lip of rock onto a wooden staircase descending some fifty feet to the chamber floor. When he reached the bottom, he strode over to Bernardo and waited behind him a moment. Bernardo didn't interrupt his work. The sword sparking and vibrating in his hand, he continued to pedal away at the big flint wheel without even looking over his shoulder.

Diego smiled again, certain Bernardo was fully aware of his presence. The family servant wasn't trying to ignore him. Not out of rudeness or ill feelings, anyway. He did things at his own pace, that was all.

At length Bernardo turned to look at him. A short, thin man in his fifties with a pouchy face, twinkling blue eyes, and a tussle of curly white hair fringing his otherwise bald scalp, he laid the sword down on a worktable beside him, offering Diego a sweet, satisfied smile.

Diego clasped his shoulder in greeting.

"Your labors on my behalf never cease, do they, old friend?" he said.

Bernardo replied using Indian sign language, touching the edge of his right hand with the thumb of his left to convey the word "sharp," then briskly slicing his right hand across his chest for "good."

"The sword's cutting edge seemed in fine enough shape to me," Diego said. "But, as always, I differ to your unerring judgement."

Gesturing rapidly, Bernardo signed that he had been to the pueblo that morning, then cupped his hand behind his ear and sketched a *Z* in the air with his index finger.

Diego grinned. "So last night's appearance by Zorro has set the pueblo abuzz. Did you hear the blackguards I put down were soldiers from the *cuartel*?"

Bernardo pulled a face, his broad, high forehead scrunching with surprise.

Diego's grin expanded. "I didn't expect Sergeant Garcia would let that embarrassing information spread very far . . . not with the new commandante, Monastario, pressuring him to whip his troops into shape so that they might finally flay the hide off The Fox."

Bernardo didn't smile, and Diego instantly found himself regretting his comment. Bernardo had served the de la Vegas since before they had resettled in Los Angeles, and been his trusted and devoted friend for as long as he could remember. He often forgot how much the poor fellow worried about him, especially with the military governor having vowed to show Zorro his tyrannical brand of justice.

"Relax, Bernardo," he said gently. "I didn't wish to make you fret with my poor choice of words. You can be sure I'll stay as far from his lancers as possible."

Bernardo stared at the younger man a little longer, then gave him a shrug, indicating he was ready to let him change the subject.

Diego was glad to do so. He was also anxious to show Bernardo the pouch.

"This was given to me a short while ago by Don Morales, a rancher from the San Fernando valley," he said, holding it out into the throw of an oil lamp.

Shifting to the edge of the stool, Bernardo leaned forward for a closer look. He took the pouch from Diego, uncinched it, glanced inside at its contents, and then raised it to his nose—almost exactly as Diego had done in his father's parlor less than an hour past.

Diego waited, allowing him to inspect it. Bernardo plucked a small clot of the substance from the pouch, smeared it between his thumb and forefinger. It left a dark stain on their tips. His eyebrows knitted together.

"What do you think?" Diego asked.

Bernardo seemed oblivious to the question. He rose suddenly from his stool, stepped past Diego, then turned left along the cave wall, walking over to a large wooden table that closely resembled the one beside the sharpening wheel.

On it was an instrument Diego had brought back from Madrid, called a microscope by men of science, and used to study objects too small to be examined by the naked eye. It consisted of two sets of adjustable lenses mounted on a hollow brass tube, a flat stage on which the glass specimen slide would be placed for viewing, and a small kerosene lamp which functioned as a light source. Invented two centuries earlier by a team of Dutch lensmakers, and further developed by Hans Kepler and other famous researchers, it had been used in countless experiments over the years, revealing the cellular construction of plants, the constituents and capillary circulation of human blood, the existence of tiny living creatures known as protozoa, and much more. In addition to having his curiosity aroused by the device, Diego had been intrigued by its potential as an investigatory tool, something that might enable one to scrutinize tiny clues left behind by malefactors—trace materials such as hair, clothing fibers, a whole range of things that could link the guilty to the evil deed, clear the innocent of suspicion, perhaps even reveal the culprit's identity in cases where it was unknown.

Bernardo, too, had been fascinated by the microscope's capabilities. The particular model Diego had purchased in Europe had cost a small fortune and been uniquely constructed by an expert who had honed the lenses to a magnification power of 300 times—outdoing the impressive technical wizardry of van Leeuwenhoek, whose microscopes had yielded images that had been 270 times the object's actual size.

Now Bernardo shook some more of the pulpy material from the pouch onto a glass slide, put the sample on the microscope's examining stage, and struck a match to light the wick of the lamp attachment. Squinting into the eyepiece, he began turning a knob to adjust its focus, then used a separate knob to do the same for the lower lens.

He moved the slide this way and that, made a few more precise adjustments to the lenses, produced a satisfied purring sound. Diego stood behind him, looking over his shoulder, watching excitement spread across his features. After a few minutes he tore his attention from the eyepiece, motioning Diego over to it, eager to share whatever he'd seen with him.

Diego leaned forward and studied the magnified specimen. Intricate details revealed themselves to him—the greenish-brown coloring and fine network of veins and geometrical cell structures that he associated with leafy plants. He noticed opaque areas where the leaf appeared to be pulverized and steeped in some sort of oily extract, or perhaps mixed with a different substance that had been prepared in that manner . . . a pounded root or bark, he guessed. But if there was some characteristic that distinguished the sample from the dozens, even hundreds of other herbal formulations Bernardo had catalogued over a lifetime of solitary research, Diego found himself at a loss as to what it might be.

He straightened, stepped away from the microscope.

"It is interesting, without a doubt . . . but unfortunately it gives away no secrets," he said. "At least to my crude eye."

Bernardo frowned severely. Diego was suddenly reminded of his days at the university, though it took him a moment to realize why: his old friend looked like a professor who'd been let down by his favorite student.

"Have I failed to grasp something that ought to be evident?" he said, trying to conceal his amusement. "If so, I hope you'll be generous with your wisdom, rather than brandish it like a paddle over a child's bottom."

Bernardo's scowling, disappointed expression became touched with irritation. Diego supposed he should have held his tongue. Why was his first reflex in these situations always sarcasm? Wasn't humility said to be the better choice?

For his part, Bernardo looked unwilling to have his patience tested any further. His forehead wrinkling, he turned his back on Diego and made his way over to an enormous footlocker against the cave wall, the sort of heavy wooden chest that might have been found in the hold of a seafaring vessel.

Diego followed him as he lifted open the lid with both hands.

The chest was filled with dozens of leather-bound books, volume upon volume heaped together in seeming disarray, many with their covers turned so the titles weren't visible—although Diego knew Bernardo was familiar with every book in the jumbled pile.

Bernardo stood for a moment, peering into the chest. Then he bent to his knees and began rummaging through the books it contained, digging them out, dusting them off, examining their spines, and unceremoniously tossing them back inside until he finally located the one he was seeking—a thick, ancient-looking volume with gilt-edged pages and baroque lettering on the cover.

Even from three feet away, Diego's keen eyes could read the title, which was in Spanish: *Jose de la Costa Aztec Herbal*.

He watched Bernardo flip quickly through its pages, then pause about halfway through the book to study an illustrated entry, his face thoughtful and serious, nodding to himself several times, totally engrossed in what he was reading.

Diego considered waiting for Bernardo to call him over—he supposed he still felt a little guilty over having offended him, and wanted to demonstrate his respect. On the other hand, his curiosity was a relentless nag.

After a few seconds he quit trying to resist it, shrugged, and came up behind him.

"So," he said. "What information have you uncovered?"

Bernardo looked at Diego, his features no longer annoyed. He passed him the open book, gestured to the page he'd been scanning. On its upper half were two side-by-side drawings, one of a stem with long, trumpet-shaped flowers, the other of a cactus with fleshy tubercles.

"*Oloiuhqui,*" Diego said in Spanish, reading aloud from the entry beneath the picture. "Sun-dried . . . disagreeable odor . . . formulated by the sacrificial priests of Moctezuma from the bark of the nightshade and *peyote,* which grows only in Mictlan, the northern desert lands . . ."

He skimmed down to the final sentence and paused, the wide circles of his eyes briefly rising to meet Bernardo's.

Bernardo stared back at him and produced a low grunt.

Diego read from the book again, feeling a chill. "When chewed or ingested, induces a twilight sleep in which one may continue to walk the earth with the living, while his soul is stolen away to the Land of the Dead . . ."

His voice trailed off a second time.

"The preparation in the medicine pouch, are you absolutely certain this is it?" he asked Bernardo after awhile.

Bernardo nodded.

Diego fell silent. So, then, one mystery had been solved. But it only raised more questions, didn't it? Baffling, terrible questions. He was no believer in magic, but if the pouch contained some sort of narcotic drug, who had given it to the so-called night walkers in whose possession it had been found? And why?

He thought about Don Morales's description of its victims and instantly knew he had to find out.

"It is good that you honed my sword to a fine edge, Bernardo," he said. "For tonight, Zorro rides again."

Chapter 4

There was an old *mestizo* saying, *"De palo caido todos quiere hacer lieña"*—"From the fallen tree everyone wants firewood"—that poignantly conveyed how it was to be a peasant living under Spanish colonial rule in the California of 1815. Downtrodden and exploited, they endured a succession of corrupt military governors whose overweening political ambition was matched only by a brittle indifference to the people's needs, and whose practice was to line their pockets by levying unfair and oppressive taxes on the most powerless of their subjects. Secure in their unaccountability to anyone but the Viceroy of Mexico, they used the armed garrisons at their command as a club, and their administrative authority as a license to wield that club as they pleased.

It was easy, then, for a thoughtful man to understand the rapid efflorescence of *Los Rayos del Sol* and its special attraction to the poor. The Indians in particular had reason to look upon the compound as a beacon of hope and sustenance. They had been decimated by measles, chicken pox, and other white man's diseases. They had been persecuted by settlers who viewed them as inferiors and found their traditional lifestyle alien and unfathomable. For a great many of them, the open-armed acceptance—as well as the generous dispensations of food, clothing, and medical treatment—they received at *Los Rayos del Sol* was far preferable to the iron dictates of Franciscan padres, who made a trip to the baptismal font and assimilation into Spanish culture a prerequisite of their charity.

There was, however, another reason the early trickle of pilgrims to the compound soon became a continuous flood. Another reason entire families would set out along the rough trails leading northward from the pueblo, leaving their adobes behind to squatters, scavengers, and scorpions, traveling on the backs of donkeys and workhorses, or crammed into dusty buckboards with their scant possessions, or marching on foot with only the clothes on their backs. Another reason they would come to *Los Rayos del Sol* by any means available, moving toward the temple pyramid in long, slow caravans, the ominous loom of its serpent totem doing nothing to discourage their progress.

In large part, they came because they had heard the settlement's founder could cure any disease, ease any pain, lift the sickness from one's body with the merest touch of his hands. Word had it that he could even assert his will over men's vices and moral failings, breaking them of habitual drunkenness and cruelty toward their wives. And after attending one of his temple gatherings they would *believe*. Some who had undertaken the trek primarily to satisfy their curiosity stayed on as devotees. Others who returned to the pueblo did so as his zealous messengers, spreading news of his wondrous deeds to friends and relatives, testifying to the incredible forcefulness of his presence and to having witnessed his acts of healing with their own eyes. He was, they said, a true mystic, a shaman of immense wisdom and power.

He was called Hidalgo el Cazador and he offered the promise of miracles.

Better still, he offered it seemingly without condition. Access to the mission was unrestricted; people were welcome to come and go as they pleased. There were no expectations of religious conversion. No pressures to substitute the figurines of ancestral gods that adorned their dwellings with the images of Christian saints. No demands to abandon their native tongues and say their prayers in the language of the colonizers. Tithes were nonexistent and donations were solicited only from the most prosperous citizens of Los Angeles, who were intrigued by how greatly Cazador had improved the living conditions of the Indians, and at whose fiestas Cazador became a valued guest— impressing the *caballeros* with tales of the distant and picturesque lands he had visited, and charming the ladies with his elegant manners, fluent conversation, and unfailing, dark-eyed attentiveness.

If there were some ulterior motive, some hidden ambition, underlying Cazador's good works, it was evident to no one. As far as could be seen his compassionate love of humanity was sincere. When people wondered aloud about the reasons for his selflessness, he would tell of having lead a life of frivolous yet somehow dissatisfying privilege until a vision of sorts had struck him, and a voice in his head—he claimed not to know whether it was his own or had sprung from some higher power—told him to go out in the world and use his great wealth to benefit the less fortunate. When this explanation led to polite questions about his origins, he spoke captivatingly of his noble Spanish heritage and descent from the conquistador Francisco Vasquez de Coronado, who had explored legendary Cibola in the sixteenth century. When asked what had brought him to California, he spoke of having heard and read a great deal about the frontier while in Mexico, each new account increasing his fascination until he decided to journey there and study it firsthand. When genteel acquaintances mentioned the fantastic curative abilities he was said to possess, he would dismiss the rumors with a smile, attributing the supposed "miracles" to his use of medicinal plants and a fair amount of exaggeration by the superstitious people he cared for. And although the information Cazador divulged about his background usually just tweaked the interest of his listeners, they were, to a person, quickly convinced of his pure intentions.

And they kept coming, the poor and the desperate, flocking to his compound in steadily increasing numbers, streaming through its walls to fall beneath the shadow of his ascendant pyramid.

"My son, he is feeling pain. Always there is so much pain."

Sitting very still, Hidalgo el Cazador studied the woman who had brought her son before him on the large rectangular platform in the temple chamber. She wore a simple homespun peasant dress and had a cotton *rebozo* over her head. Though clean, the dress was threadbare, and showed the seams and patches of frequent mending. The lines of stitching were uneven and made the fabric bunch up where some of the larger holes had been sewn closed. Her hands were rough, with fingers that thickened around the knuckles, and had greyish callouses on their tips. The skin on her heavy face was dry and leathery. If vanity had ever been part of her character makeup, a life of hardship had eroded any perceptible trace of it.

"You see his arm, how it twists to one side. So that he cannot move it, or stand up with his back straight," she said. "Sometimes he cries in his bed at night. I sit with him but can do nothing and his crying does not stop until the sun comes into the sky."

She spoke quietly in an imprecise and halting Spanish, tilting her head down to avert her eyes from the man in front of her, her posture typical of so many who came to his daily assemblies. While not quite defeated it was meek and abject, as if she had learned that the cost of survival in the Spanish Dominion was an attitude of cringing obeisance. He continued looking at her. The Indians had sacrificed their ferocious independence, allowed it to be bred out of them, and for what? Scraps and bones, picked over throwaways, he thought. They were to their distant ancestors what leashed dogs were to wolves.

He remembered how magnificent they had been in bygone times, and was sickened to see the tame and servile creatures they had become.

"What is the boy's name?" he asked.

"Joaquin."

"No," he said, his tone edged with impatience.

"Look up and give me his true name. Not the one by which he is known to the *pobladores* of the Conquest."

She raised her head, but only a little, and only for a moment, her eyes flicking onto his face and then lowering again in supplication.

"Running Antelope," she said in the language of the Yang Na tribe.

He nodded slowly and gazed past her at the crowd that had gathered in the audience chamber. There were perhaps a hundred ragtag men, women, and children waiting for the chance to address him, a solid mass of bodies that stretched back to the chamber entrance from the foot of his platform. The near-total silence in the hall seemed to throb with their need and expectation. Now and then the stillness would be disturbed by an anticipant murmur, but the sounds were quickly damped by the thick mague tapestries draping the walls.

He looked again at the woman in front of him. "Your son . . . has he suffered from this affliction since birth?"

She shook her head; dropping a coarse but tender hand onto the back of the boy's neck.

He was about nine or ten years old, with a small oval face, brown eyes, and olive skin. While the right side of his body seemed normal, his left was at least partially crippled—his shoulder drooping, his arm hooked at the elbow and hanging dead against his middle, his fingers curled into a paralytic claw. His leg on that side was rigid and stiltlike.

"Until one year ago, Don Cazador, he was like any other boy. But he went climbing in a place where he had been warned not to go, and fell from high up on a bluff, and got hurt very bad. Some men from the village found him and carried him back to my adobe. He did not move for days afterward, and burned with a fever, and many in my village believed that he would die. They told me I should be ready for this, but I did not listen to their words. I cared for him, and made him drink root medicine, and each day he got stronger by a little. His spirit did not leave him. But when he rose from his bed, he was as he is now."

He was quiet as the woman spoke, the full weight of his gaze resting upon her careworn features. When she was finished with her story, he nodded at the boy, who was clinging nervously to her side.

"Step closer," he said in a low voice.

The boy glanced up at his mother, hesitating.

Still leaning forward, Cazador reached an arm out from under his cloak and took hold of the little boy's shoulder.

"Come here, child. There's no reason to fear me."

The boy continued staring at his mother, his eyes anxious and overbright. She gave him a nod of encouragement, placed her hand against the small of his back, and gently urged him toward Cazador.

His resistance lasted another moment before finally dissipating. Still, he approached Cazador without ease or confidence, his gait crooked, his bad leg dragging over the tiled platform, every movement a struggle.

Cazador again became aware of the silence around him as he studied the boy's face . . . a waiting, expansive silence that pressed against the chamber walls as if it were trying to burst out into the wider world.

"Your name is a good name," he said, raising his voice to a volume that he knew would carry to the far end of the hall. His eyes burned into the boy.

"They say nothing alive is faster than the antelope. Did you know this?"

The boy nodded.

"They say a person is named after an animal because he shares its qualities. Is that true of yourself? Were your legs once able to outrun those of other young ones in your village?"

The boy's reaction to the question was immediate and pronounced. His eyes teared over with the memory of lost physical capabilities. Of how it had felt to be an ordinary child with ordinary limitations. He opened and closed his mouth as if he were about to say something, but in the end could find no words to encompass the emotions bulging up inside him and simply gave Cazador another nod.

"I can make you well, but I will need your faith in this," Cazador said. He leaned closer to the boy, keeping a firm grip on his shoulder with the long, tapered fingers of his right hand. His other hand appeared from under the heavy folds of his cloak and closed around the boy's left shoulder. "What do you say?"

The boy stared at Cazador in the silence of the hall. Behind him, his mother watched both of them raptly, the lines deepening on her face.

"Will you give me the trust that I need to do my work?" Cazador asked. His arms were unyielding bars on either side of the boy's neck.

The boy looked around at his mother's hopeful face, then shifted his eyes back to Cazador and slowly nodded a third time.

"Good," Cazador said.

He pulled the boy closer, dropping his right hand from where it had rested on his shoulder, sliding it under his shirt, spreading his fingers over his ribcage.

The boy shivered involuntarily but did not pull away. Cazador's hand moved around to his back and pressed down on the middle of his twisted spine.

The boy's trembling became more intense. His face raddled with color. A shiny film of perspiration appeared on his forehead. He inhaled and exhaled with hard, percussive breaths.

"Tonatiuh quautlevanitl," Cazador said in a tongue that only one at the foot of the platform recognized. But, as he'd expected, the strangeness of it only seemed to heighten the crowd's attention. The packed bodies below him had been fused into a single captive organism, and it was his to command.

"The sun, eagle," Cazador intoned, shifting to Spanish so they would understand him, offering a little bait to lead them toward deeper mystery. "Make us glow, send us your darts of fire."

The boy was breathing rapidly, almost panting now, the sweat pouring down his face. The flush had crept from his cheeks to his neck and forehead.

"Accept what I offer," Cazador said. His eyes were locked with the boy's. "Open yourself to illumination and be healed."

A thin reedy sound issued from the boy's mouth. He tossed his head back spasmodically, the pulse points fluttering on either side of his neck. His eyes rolled up under their lids so that only their whites were visible. Some of those watching would later claim they heard the air crackle around him and saw the hair raise off his scalp in a sort of crown, almost like rays of sunlight.

And then his misshapen left hand began to twitch with life, his hooked fingers unlocking, stretching apart. His head shook from side to side, still hanging limply backward from his neck. His face was a bright crimson. The sounds escaping his lips had strung together into low, quavery moans.

Behind him his mother stood frozen with a contradictory mixture of terror, joy, and rapturous awe, watching as his hand was released from its paralysis, watching the painful bow of his spine straighten from his hips up to his shoulders, watching her son convulse in the burning, scouring grip of a miracle.

"With the power I possess you will be *healed*!" Cazador intoned.

Now he rose from his chair and pulled the little boy to his chest, wrapping both arms around him. His hands flattened between the boy's shoulder blades, one atop the other, their fingers splayed. His cloak poured over the boy, shrouding him from sight.

"Yes, child, yes. Be whole and free of pain," Cazador said, his deep voice filling the chamber.

A moment passed.

Another.

The boy remained enfolded in the cloak. To many in the spellbound crowd it looked as if he had been swallowed up by it, as if he were no longer there in front of them at all. But then Cazador opened his hands and spread them wide above his head, the cloak parting, swirling back from around the boy like a dark mist in a rush of wind.

The boy stood in place between Cazador and his mother, stood tall and straight, both arms relaxed at his sides, the feverish color gone from his cheeks. His eyes a little disoriented, he raised the arm that had been frozen and useless since his fall from the bluff so many months before, raised it up to examine it, and slowly flexed his hand—balling it into a fist, then unclenching his fingers. He did this twice, than again, each time with less stiffness, taking pleasure in the simple repetitive action while seeming wary of disappointment . . . as if he suspected that he'd somehow fallen into a dream, that he could not possibly be doing what he thought he was doing, and that the sensations of restored movement he was feeling would prove to be wickedly false.

At last, the reality of it all sank in, and a huge smile lit his face. He lowered his hand and took two steps toward his mother, his limp gone, his left leg moving in smooth coordination with his right.

Halfway through his third step she released an ecstatic cry and snatched him to her arms, hugging him against her breast. The previously silent crowd took up and amplified her reaction, filling the chamber with incredulous gasps and wild, elated shouts. Usually stolid ranch hands, men hardened by years of toil and subjugation, applauded and slapped each other's backs. Many of the women were laughing and weeping at the same time.

Tears spilling down her creased, wrinkled face, the boy's mother approached Cazador and started to speak—but, like her son minutes earlier, she was overcome with emotion and couldn't manage it.

She cleared her throat, swallowed, fighting to control herself.

"What can I give you for this great thing you have done?" she asked finally, the boy still in her embrace. "Anything I have is yours—"

He stopped her with a wave of his hands, his black eyes very sharp. "Go from here without debt or obligation, señora. I want nothing but to know your child is well. In days to come he will run like his namesake, his body and spirit once again in harmony."

For a moment she just stood there in tearful gratitude. Then she lowered the boy to his feet, approached Cazador, took his hand in both her own, and kissed it with a reverent, almost girlishly shy bow.

After that she quickly straightened, turned, put her arm around her son, and walked with him to the three broad steps leading down from the platform.

The crowd swept around them as they reached the chamber floor and started toward the entrance, jamming in close, their euphoria swelling up like a river that has overflowed its banks.

Cazador watched them for a moment, watched all of them, his eyes roving over their excited faces, a small, secret smile touching the corners of his lips:

Then he turned with a whisk of his cloak, strode into the archway beside his chair, and left the chamber.

The figure stood just under twelve inches high and occupied a small nook in a corner of the room. Subtle variations of blue and green showed on its translucent jade surfaces, giving it an almost liquid aspect . . . a contradictory impression that was one of many at its essence. Combining the features of a jaguar and a human infant, the object blended innocence and feral savagery, and was at once beautiful for its workmanship and hideous for what it represented—a creature that belonged in the darkest of nightmares, an atrocity against everything that was sane and natural and *right* in the world. The eyes above the cherubic roundness of its cheeks were cruel and sharp, their pupils the vertical slits of a nocturnal predator. Two spiking, carnivorous fangs extruded from its lower jaw, pushing back the soft curve of its chin, warping its lips into a swollen grimace. Its short, plump arms—folded over its breast like those of a newborn clutching its swaddling blanket—resolved into claws below the wrists.

Hidalgo el Cazador studied the jade changeling in silence, his back to the arch through which he had strode from the audience chamber, the celebratory cries of his flock echoing in the passage behind it.

He contemplatively rubbed his thin beard with one hand. The years had not dimmed his admiration for the lapidary who had worked the idol's features out of hard stone, not in the slightest. His name had been Tizoc, he remembered. Born a slave, his skills with the greenstone had earned him unequaled prestige in the floating city, imperial Tenochtitlan.

Cazador moved forward in the room's wavery torchlight, reaching for the statue, his elongated shadow scaling the mudbrick wall behind him.

Yes, he remembered.

Tizoc.

A slight, ascetic man who had kept his own company and gone obsessively about his business. Known for his patience and genius, the artistry he put into each piece, the diligence with which he had labored over every expressive detail. His creations were much sought after by the priests, mediums, sorcerers and blood-soaked necromancers of the high court, but the time-consuming demands of his craft were such that he would accept commissions from very few of them ... and then only after extracting a huge pile of gold ingots for his efforts.

"Even Moctezuma himself met your price without bickering," Cazador whispered under his breath, his lips tightening around the name of the long-dead war-lord as if he had tasted of something vile. "Indeed, Tizoc, this exquisite thing of your making has out-lasted that weak, pampered fool by many centuries. Long after his cowardice brought the great darkness upon our people, long after his bones crumbled to dry dust, its power endures. As does mine . . . and therein is a lesson about the value of time and planning, I think."

He took the statue from its niche and held it up to the cast of the torch, turning and turning it in his hands. Veins of cold emerald fire pulsed through its depths in lacy, intertwining patterns.

"Time and planning," he repeated, thinking of his little performance in the audience chamber. Everything had been exactly right. The passionate yearning of the crowd, their desire and willingness to believe . . . and the easily treatable nature of the boy's con-dition. He'd had no broken bones, no physical defect inherited from his forebears. Nothing that should have permanently disabled him. What he had needed was only an *adjustment* of sorts.

Of course the words Cazador had spoken to him in Nahuatl, the language of his vanished people, had nothing to do with restoring the boy to normalcy. Nor had that been accomplished with some mystical laying on of hands. Rather, Cazador had applied a science with ancient origins in China, where he had sojourned long ago, and where a healer called Li Chan had charged out the lines of vital force, called *qi,* that ran through the body. Li Chan had seen a relation be-tween these flow-lines and the physical condition of his patients, teaching that good health resulted when the flow was in balance, that sickness arose when it became blocked at certain critical points, and that relief for a patient's ills might be accomplished by exerting pressure upon—or painlessly inserting needles *into*—those chokepoints, clearing them just as a dam or some other obstruction might be cleared from a stream that has been diverted from its course, allowing the energy to flow uninterrupted. Cazador had seen Li Chan's system demonstrated by practitioners of great talent, and had himself studied with them for a time, learning what he could of their techniques.

Cazador looked at the statue another moment before returning it to its place. Though cool to his touch on the outside, there was a pulsing warmth underneath, soft but discernable, as if it were a chrysalis filled with mysterious, incubating life.

Science. Magic. The Spanish feared the latter, extolled the former. For the Indians, the opposite was true. How foolish, since the disciplines were separated by gossamer-thin veils and often could be complimentary . . . as what had happened in the audience chamber went to show. While one had made the boy whole, the other had bound the boy to the statue, the statue to the boy, and both to Cazador.

A wan smile stole across his lips as he replaced the statue and turned back into the archway. Much lay ahead of him this day, including an interesting little engagement that he planned to make shortly before sundown.

A tool was a tool, was it not?

Each to its own purpose, and valuable in its own way.

He would put all of his to good use in days to come.

Chapter 5

Arcadia Flores lay atop her peasant's bed, her face buried in the blanket spread across its straw matting— a bed cover that she had spun from raw wool with her own hands, and that was now stained dark with her freshly spilled tears. She could feel the wetness of those tears against her cheeks as they soaked into the heavy woven fabric, could hear the rhythmic, muffled hitching of her sobs in the otherwise unbroken silence of the hut, and wished she could somehow pull herself together, somehow make the crying *stop*. She knew she had to be strong for the sake of her loved ones . . . but, in fairness to herself, had simply endured too much in too short a period of time to keep her emotions bottled up inside.

Yes, if the tears must come, she thought, then let them come now and be finished, so that she could decide what needed to be done, and move forward with clear eyes and a clearer head. It was best to do her weeping in private and present a resolute face to the world.

And yet . . .

And yet she had been raised in a household where the sound of such unhappiness would be immediately met with soothing words from one of her parents— and even from her brother, who had always treated her with affection in spite of his self-conscious and unintentionally comical machismo. Tonight, however, she had only the bare, whitewashed walls of the adobe for company. Walls that once had been full of warmth and comfort, providing refuge from any hardship that might arrive by way of the outside world. Walls that now stood as stark reminders of everything she had lost. She ached, physically *ached*, with a terrible sense of loneliness and vulnerability that had settled into her bones like an ague.

Her father and brother were gone, lured away to *Los Rayos del Sol*, taking their modest possessions with them, leaving her with nothing except her terror and confusion . . . and the empty, forsaken silence in which both would bloom and ripen as the long night wore on.

And with one other thing as well, Arcadia thought, sniffling into her blanket. *A memory I fear will still be clinging to me when my face is wrinkled with age, my hair is grey and thin, and most other recollections have dimmed from my mind.*

She again pictured Hidalgo el Cazador standing outside the hut's open door. Pictured the sharp, expectant, *greedy* look in his eyes, like that of a hawk about to spiral in toward its prey. Pictured it and felt an icy shiver rattle through her spine.

He had been waiting.

Waiting for *her,* and no one else.

She had known it the moment she saw him upon her return from the market . . . had it only been several hours ago? It was hard to believe, perhaps because the day started out so unexceptionally. Indeed, up until that point it merely had been busy and exhausting.

Arcadia's experience with the costumed rogues the night before had not dissuaded her from setting up her stall in the plaza; work was work, and she could not have afforded the loss of any trade to competitive sellers. Furthermore, the men that had threatened her were locked away behind bars thanks to El Zorro, and she had seen no danger in going about her business. Just to be on the cautious side, she had left the plaza an hour earlier than had been her habit in the past several weeks, hoping to make it back home while some daylight remained in the sky.

Along the way she had fallen into an introspective and somewhat troubled mood, riding with her harness ropes loosely in hand and the oxen making their deliberate, plodding way up the well-worn path. Much had been changing for her in recent weeks, and it was easy to trace every one of the changes to the coming of *Los Rayos del Sol.* Having heard much talk about it, her father and brother had first visited the mission some weeks back, eager to see it for themselves. Like many others—*hundreds* of others, she guessed—they had left there brewing with excitement over the spiritual rewards it seemed to offer and made frequent return visits. At first, Arcadia had seen no reason to be suspicious of its magnetic founder and sage, Hidalgo el Cazador—no more than she was of so-called holy men in general, at any rate. While it was true that the majority of *Cristiano* friars were as short on kindness and compassion as they were doggedly insistant about telling others how to live, what tongue to speak, and which gods it was permissable to worship, for some, the reward of helping fellow human beings was all there was to it . . . and Cazador had given every indication of being one of the latter. He received the people that arrived at his camp with unconditional respect and charity. He gave shelter to the homeless, remedies to the sick, and sent the starving back to their villages with full stomachs and meal packages for their families. He took in broken-spirited *Indios* who had drowned themselves in tequila and *pulque* and broke them of their consuming addictions.

Even now Arcadia could not deny this, not any more than she could deny the difference she had seen in her father and Antonio after their earliest trips to the mission. For months after the accident that killed Arcadia's mother, she had feared she might soon lose her remaining parent as well; a man who had weathered many difficult trials in his time, Lorenzo Flores had grown morose and disengaged from even the most routine affairs, as if the weight of the world had become too much to bear without his wife to help him support it. And although her brother Antonio's temperament had remained vigorous and easygoing on the surface, she had seen a similar darkness in his eyes during unguarded moments.

Arcadia hadn't known what had been done to mend their spirits at *Los Rayos del Sol*, but it was obvious that *something* had helped lift them from despair, and she had been so pleased and amazed by this that she had deliberately ignored the warnings of her heart . . . warnings that might have told her that not all was right with either of the two men. That a great deal, in fact, was very wrong.

Ah, but some part of me must have sensed the truth, she thought now. *For why else didn't I accompany them in their rides out to the mission, although Papa often begged me to come along?*

She supposed the answer to that question was moot, and what good was there in turning up old soil for it anyway? Her end she had been unable to dismiss her misgivings, and when it came to such things later was better than never. The reality she had finally confronted was this: while her brother and father had seemed more alive after their pilgrimages, they had scarcely thrown themselves back into the ordinary business of *living*. Instead they centered themselves around Hidalgo el Cazador, showing enthusiasm only when they spoke of him, neglecting their work, drifting away again and again to assist in ongoing construction at the mission compound, lingering at his camp until it reached a point at which she rarely saw them at all. At the dinner table, where the family had always gathered at the close of the day, and around which the conversation had once spun so energetically it was difficult to get a word in edgewise (less after her mother died, it was true, though Antonio had had his talkative moments even in the depths of his grief) Arcadia had often found herself eating alone. In recent weeks, as the absences of her father and brother had grown longer, and the silences in her home deeper, Arcadia had tried to push aside her concerns by concentrating on simple everyday chores and her work at the loom . . . there had, after all, been a great many rugs and garments to complete in preparation for the carnival. But her concerns had refused to be pushed aside, and just recently she had promised herself that she would travel out to *Los Rayos del Sol* after the holiday had passed, hoping to obtain a better understanding of the place—and the man—that seemed to have spellbound Lorenzo and Antonio.

However, fate has a way of putting one's plans at a radical tilt, and then upending them again before a person can regain his or her balance. So fully did Hidalgo el Cazador occupy her thoughts, Arcadia had almost come to regard him as a real but unseen presence in her life, hovering over her every waking moment . . . and many of her dreaming ones as well. But he had been absolutely the last person on earth she had expected to see as she'd neared the adobe she shared with her father and brother, urging her span of draft oxen over the twisting, uphill trail from the pueblo.

Nor was his presence the only surprise that had been awaiting her.

For several heartbeats after the oxen crested the rise on which her home was built, she sat as a woman suspended in time, caught between one second and the next. Behind the adobe, the setting sun had plunged toward its nadir, its red-orange dusklight making it appear as if the western hills were dissolving in flame. With the smoldering sky in the background, and his shadow stretched long in front of him, the stranger whose identity she would quickly guess might have come striding from a vast sea of fire that had blanketed the horizon from north to south.

Then her gaze had swept to the left, where a horse cart had been pulled between the adobe and the barnyard. Behind the corral's fence, the chickens were squawking and fluttering excitedly, and her family's small handful of sheep were lined up against the wooden poles, peering at the wagon with bright, frightened eyes, bleating like gossipy, white-stockinged Spanish matrons who had gathered to watch a public row.

What Arcadia saw—*who* she saw—in the wagon's rear made her gasp audibly in horror and disbelief.

"No," she muttered. *"Mis ojos fal doritos."*

But however she wished it were otherwise, her eyes surely were not deceiving her.

Surrounded by large sacks of what she would later discover were their gathered possessions, her father and brother stared in Arcadia's direction from the box of the wagon. Neither gave any sign that they recognized her, but merely sat slumped and unmoving amid the piled-up canvas bags, as if they had fallen asleep with their eyes wide open.

Her whole body trembling, Arcadia glanced at the front of the wagon and took in the two men occupying the driver's seat. Massively built and wearing only spotted animal pelts, both were facing straight ahead, away from her, toward the rough downhill trail winding down to Alondra Creek, and then continuing southward to the valley of San Fernando, perhaps an hour's ride away.

"Be at ease, your *endidas* come with me freely. It is their wish to participate in a grand, good work."

Arcadia turned toward the man who had spoken those words, regarding him with bewilderment and dismay, jerking on her line to halt the oxen in their tracks. Though she had never before laid eyes on him, she felt instantly certain that it was Hidalgo el Cazador who stood midway between herself and the open entrance to her home, speaking in a deep, resonant voice that commanded her full attention, watching her closely as the sun burned itself out behind him.

Nearly a full minute passed. Arcadia could think of no response, could barely think *at all*. Numb with shock, certain she would be incapable of saying anything coherent, she sat helplessly before him, her mind pitching and yawing like a ship in a storm. For a while she almost felt as if she would remain there forever with her hands clenched tightly around the harness rope and speech having deserted her . . . but the contrast between the cloaked man's bright, purposeful gaze and the lackluster stares of her father and brother was finally to much to bear in silence.

"Freely? It does not appear so to me," she said. She looked over at them again, and the blank, complacent expressions their faces brought up something close to hysteria in her. "*Papa, Antonio—*"

"They will not answer," Cazador interrupted suddenly. "They cannot."

"What is wrong with them?" she said, fighting back tears. "What have you *done* to them?"

"All can be explained, señorita, if we could only speak to each other as friends. But that seems impossible while you remain where you are, and I stand at your doorstep and await your proper greeting."

Like the devil himself, Arcadia thought, her heart thudding in her chest. *And no sooner would I approach you than him.*

"It does not seem my invitation has been needed thus far," she said, and nodded toward the adobe's open door. "For I see you have already welcomed yourself to our home, and taken what you wished from us, Don Cazador." She swallowed, adding: "If my guess is correct, and that is who you are."

A smile slanted thinly across his face. Arcadia thought he might have intended it to be benign or reassuring, but it failed miserably on both counts.

"It is the name by which I am known," he said. "Why, though, do you speak it with such harshness? Such anger?"

Arcadia regarded him, still trying not to cry, her knuckles white around the harness line. Anger? Yes, here was a feeling she had not even felt taking shape, leaving him to recognize it before she did. Here it was, thrusting up through her fear like a sharp jut of stone, jagged and unlovely—but also *hard,* and something she could hang onto.

She decided to ignore his question and ask one of her own instead, anticipating his answer, but wanting to have it laid out openly between them.

"Where do you take my father and brother?" she said.

"The Mission," he said, still smiling like a cat that had discovered a nest of unguarded hatchlings. "They will be fine there."

"If so, then only after being herded off like animals," Arcadia said, her lips trembling. She felt trickles of wetness on her cheeks at last, but realized that they were tears of rage more than anything else . . . and that she felt increasingly in control of herself despite those tears. "I ask you again, what has been done to rob them of their senses?"

Cazador fixed her with a look of narrow appraisal.

"You are . . . a woman to be admired," he said, avoiding her question. "I see this very clearly."

And I see just as clearly that you are a man to be

feared beyond all others, she thought, her arms and shoulders erupting into gooseflesh.

"Come, Arcadia Flores," he said slowly, his eyes boring into hers. "Join your loved ones."

She watched him silently. Dusk had gathered around them, leaving only a few crimson spears of sunlight to pierce the sky above the hills. Briefly, his eyes seemed to catch their fire and glow like live embers in a bed of ashes.

"Join *me,*" he said, and reached his hand out in front of him, palm up, as if expecting Arcadia to dismount her wagon and take hold of it.

She watched him in the fading daylight.

Her eyes unable to leave his eyes.

His eyes giving off a heat that seemed to sweep across the distance between them in radiating waves.

She watched him. The heat, *his* heat, rising in her, creeping up her thighs, her belly, the swell of her breasts. Swirling through her brain until she was almost delirious with it.

"Come," he said.

His eyes holding her.

"Come."

Arcadia wiped her brow, sweating despite the cool evening breeze. Merciful Heaven, the heat, the consuming *heat,* what was he doing to her?

"Come."

She looked down at her hands as if from afar, saw them relax their grip on the harness, saw herself swing a leg over the side of the wagon . . .

And put every ounce of her will into stopping herself from going any further.

"Come to me now."

"Leave me be. I beg of you. I—"

"*Now.*"

His eyes. Holding. That red light filling their sockets, blazing from their sockets.

Dizzy, short of breath, she suddenly felt the last of her resistance melting away, found herself hoping Cazador would *not* leave her at all, felt herself wanting to be with him in spite of her pleas to the contrary, right there before the eyes of her father, right there in the gathering night, urgently, sinfully, there, right *there*, with him, in the open, submitting to him in a way that would flush all fear and reason from her mind, allowing the heat to incinerate her.

Arcadia would never be sure what spared her, only that something broke their connection at the very moment she would have gone to him, given herself to him, lost herself to him.

Something broke their connection, yes. His eyes wavered, the red glow going out of them. She saw his head crane up and slightly outward like that of a wolf sniffing the breeze for a scent, then felt the strength, the *need,* leave her, and fell back in the seat of the wagon, panting as if she had just run a mile at full pace.

Something, she thought. Something. And whatever it was, she knew she would be eternally grateful for it.

"Ah, my brothers," he said distantly. And then, seeming to speak to himself, continued with words that were even more baffling: "Wait. Watch. I see with your eyes, *jagueros.*"

Arcadia slumped in her wagon seat, gasping for breath, her head swimming. If someone had happened upon the scene at that instant, she was certain she would have looked as blank and empty as her brother and father, with only the spilled tears on her cheeks betraying her inner turmoil.

"This is a night for first encounters, and there is one of great importance awaiting me at the mission," Cazador said looking straight at Arcadia now. His eyes large and black, making her wonder whether she'd but imagined the strange fire in them. "We will have opportunity to finish what has been started here. I promise you."

She required a huge effort of will to croak out her response: *"Go."*

Cazador regarded her, surprise mixing with wonder on his face. Regarded her steadily, so that she began to fear he would exert his unnatural pull over her again, storming past her resistance with a power that defied her comprehension.

Instead he tossed back his head, placed his hands over his middle, and produced a laugh that sounded like the dry scraping of desert stones.

The laughter was the last thing Arcadia heard before she passed out.

When she came to, her body sprawled limply across her seat, the oxen incredibly still standing where she had halted them in front of her adobe, there were stars in the sky, and she was alone . . . unless one counted the animals lazily poking about the corral for something to eat. Having missed their late afternoon feeding, the interest they'd had in what was going on outside the fence had given way to hunger.

Cazador, his men, her father and brother . . .

All of them were gone.

Arcadia had taken a few moments to gather her wits, then climbed down from the cart and walked dazedly toward the hut . . . entering to find it not only abandoned, but stripped very close to bare. Everything of any value whatsoever—her family's riding equipment, their rifles, their scant keepsakes—had been removed, presumably bundled away in the sacks she had seen in the rear of Cazador's wagon. It was as though the place had been ransacked.

Which, she supposed, really was not that far from the truth.

Now, many hours later, she raised her head off her bed and swiped a hand across her bloodshot eyes, determined to staunch the flow of her tears, thinking that the time for crying was past. Indeed, she had wept through the night, and now that darkness was lifting, there was too much waiting ahead of her for any thought of sleep. If there was one thing she had learned from her brief but terrible encounter with Hidalgo el Cazador, it was that he could make human beings jerk to his will as if they were puppets on invisible strings. And although she did not know what to make of that unspeakable ability, her experience with it had left her feeling ashamed and violated. Indeed, it was difficult to say which was worse—the inexpressible sense of vulnerability, of no longer being quite able to *trust* herself, or her dread over what might happen to her father and brother unless they were somehow freed from Cazador's control.

But she could give those questions her consideration some other time. Her immediate plan was to ride for the pueblo at dawn and call upon Sergeant Garcia. While he was far from the most effective of law officers—to put it kindly—she supposed even he would be capable of recognizing that something was very wrong at *Los Rayos del Sol* once she'd told her tale.

And should she fail to convince him . . . well, she would not let herself worry about that, not now. There was too much waiting ahead of her.

She would go see Garcia, and give him a chance to hear her out. After that . . .

If she had learned anything in her life, it was that time would bring about its own unpredictable conclusions.

Chapter 6

The full moon was nearing its zenith when Zorro
reached the outskirts of the Indian camp, having
urged Tornado over hillsides and down valley trails
for many hours, riding southward into the woodlands
beyond the cultivated groves of the ranchos. Behind
him, the air was redolent of citrus; here the perfume
blanketing the rugged landscape was of wilder things,
lilac and golden poppies and the waxen bloom of the
yucca.

Just as Don Morales had told him—or had told
Diego de la Vega, at any rate—the trail cut by the
mysterious tribesman was a broad avenue running toward their hutted camp, flanked by white oaks and
cottonwoods whose branches broke the moonlight
into glowing splinters. The pyramid that loomed up
ahead was also mostly true to Morales's description.
Dwarfing even the tallest trees, it was adorned with

lifelike, carved-stone jaguars that seemed to circle its ascending tiers in bold procession. Zorro could see long flights of stairs on two sides of the magnificent structure. They climbed several hundred feet to where it abruptly ended in a rectangular platform, on top of which stood a stone idol representing some fierce, mythical creature . . . a plumed serpent, its mouth gaping and fanged.

Now Zorro halted Tornado and regarded the edifice rising from the valley floor with fascination. The statue perched on its flattened peak wasn't something one was likely to forget. Surely it must have been raised after Morales's second and last journey into the area. How else could he have failed to mention it, while so faithfully recounting the other details of what he'd come upon here?

Zorro pulled Tornado's reins to the left, urging the black stallion off the trail. He did not want to chance being discovered by those whom he wished to observe. Better to take advantage of whatever concealment was available.

Dismounting, Zorro found a gap where he could enter the underbrush and led Tornado into the shadows beneath the treetops. He continued to approach the Indian camp in silence, steering his horse around tangled patches of vegetation, pausing occasionally to listen to the sounds of the night . . . the hoot of an owl, the chirruping of insects, the rustlings of small rodents and lizards through the leafy ground cover.

Nothing outstanding or unusual. The Fox was in his element.

Zorro's lips tightened at the thought. It had a nicely comforting ring, didn't it? Yet, on review, he had to admit it contradicted all his deeper instincts. Why was he so ill at ease?

He kept on a little further and then paused again, looking carefully toward the camp. He estimated that he was about two hundred feet from its outer edge but still couldn't see much of anything through the foliage.

He'd have to get closer.

He moved forward, Tornado's hooves crunching over the ground behind him. After a few more yards, however, he felt the horse suddenly pull up short. Holding the bridle, he turned and placed a hand on its muscular neck. Tornado grunted and snorted, remaining visibly and uncharacteristically distressed.

Zorro's eyes narrowed behind the slits of his mask as he stroked the horse's mane. He still hadn't managed to push off his own unease . . . a sense that he was not alone, that there was something, some kind of threatening presence. Since donning the guise of the Fox he'd come to trust and even rely on such feelings, for what were they but warning signals triggered by his highest perceptions? As a Yang Na shaman had once told him, the eyes and ears could reveal a great deal to the mind without one's conscious awareness.

He stood silent and unmoving. There were more insectile chirps and creaks. More skittering noises in the undergrowth. The breeze shivered the leaves of a nearby tree. And then he heard a new sound coming from ahead of him. From the direction of the camp. One that was both immediately recognizable and completely surprising. Could it really be what it seemed?

He gave Tornado's reins a gentle tug and pushed through the thicket. Despite his anxiety, the horse hesitated just a moment longer, then followed without further coaxing. Tornado was brave and unfailingly loyal, as Zorro had known he would·be the first time he'd seen the horse running free, leading the herd through the rugged countryside beyond his father's ranch. He doubted there was any danger into which Tornado would not willingly accompany him.

Slowly, quietly, he reached out and parted the brush.

A stunned exhalation hissed through his teeth.

"My God," he muttered.

A stone wall had been built around the camp, perhaps fifteen feet high in places, much lower where construction still appeared to be in its early stages. Zorro had come stealing up near one of those unfinished sections—a stroke of good fortune for which he was grateful indeed, since it gave him an open view of the field it encircled. Spread across the clearing were at least a hundred raggedly clothed laborers. Some stooped beneath the weight of the huge clay bricks they were carrying on their shoulders. Others worked at the ground with crude picks and shovels. Their faces were blank and empty, their eyes locked in front of them. Dust covered their skeletal bodies and rose around them in a thin haze. None of them deviated from their tasks as they brought their arms up and down, up and down, resembling machines more than living men.

Zorro took in a breath. What he'd heard in the thicket was the sound of their tools cutting into the rocky earth. The camp was expanding and being fortified at an astonishing pace ... and it seemed that those doing the work in the manner of automatons, the moon providing their only light, were the night-walkers of whom Don Morales had spoken.

He peered from behind the low-hanging tree limbs with raw horror and amazement, scarcely able to believe his eyes. Striding rigidly among the laborers were stout, well-built men who looked as if they might be guards or overseers. Clad in jaguar pelts that left their muscular chests bare, their dark square-cut hair falling to their shoulders, they moved about the camp carrying whips and javelins and heavy clubs. There were knives in scabbards at their waists.

Zorro switched his gaze back to the pyramid, switched it again to a wide plot of ground that had been cleared some yards from the base of the steps. A work crew there was moving large masonry building blocks and guiding them into place over logrolls. And watching them from the pyramid's uppermost height, his back to the monstrous serpent totem, was the tall, cloaked form of a man.

Zorro gazed at the figure in surprise, wondering how he could have missed seeing him atop the pyramid in the first place. It was, of course, possible the man had emerged from inside it while he'd been looking elsewhere. In fact that was the likely explanation. But his sudden appearance was only part of what had snared Zorro's attention. There was something about his erect bearing, the lift of his chin, the detached vigilance with which he surveyed the activity below him. Something very much out of the ordinary. As the son of a prominent member of the community, he had spent many hours among men of stature and power. He knew how they carried themselves, and had no doubt that he was looking at someone of great importance in the camp—perhaps even its leader.

Zorro didn't have long to ponder this—only seconds, in fact, before the man turned to look in his direction. It was a moment he would rue in times to come, marking it as his introduction to an old, dark force that was as close to pure evil as anything he'd ever known, a force that would tear through his life like a ravaging whirlwind.

Now, though, he was merely baffled by his own absolute certainty that he'd been spotted. It didn't seem rational, not any more than to think the man on the pyramid could have been aware he was being watched. There were a good many yards between them, and the darkness and underbrush provided him with ample cover. Zorro knew he should have been hidden from sight and in any other situation would have felt confident that he was. And yet he had felt the man's eyes make contact with him.

Far across the moonlit camp, the cloaked figure remained motionless, gazing off toward the thicket from his lofty vantage.

Zorro took another breath and released it, once again telling himself he was thinking the impossible. But the feeling that he was being studied would not be negated. It was a sensation he did not know how to describe, and might not have wished to even if he could. It was almost as though invisible hands were thrusting out at him, searching him, trying to reach deep inside his brain.

Now Tornado produced another grunt and began to stamp the ground. Breaking his eyes away from the cloaked figure, Zorro glanced over his shoulder at the stallion. His thick mane was bristling, his head tossing jerkily from side to side. He started to wonder whether Tornado had shared his disquieting sense of being watched from afar, but then a sound in the brush abruptly made him realize the horse was reacting to something very different.

Something was moving on his left.

Zorro crouched in the darkness and listened. The moonlight was throwing devious shadows across the growth of trees and scrub brush around him, making his vision unreliable. He would have to be guided by what he heard rather than what he saw.

He breathed quietly. A moment passed. Another. The sound repeated itself but this time seemed to come from his opposite side. Then from his left again.

It seemed he had not one, but two unseen companions.

He waited. There was another surge of movement on the right. Louder now. Closer. Branches bent and were pushed aside. Twigs snapped on the ground.

He turned to investigate the latest sounds, his hand falling over the hilt of his sword. There was more crashing as whatever was stalking him rushed to within a foot or two away.

And then he heard it

Zorro felt the skin prickle along his spine and willed himself to stay calm.

He peered into the thicket

The pair of slitted eyes staring back at him glowed eerily through the chaparral, red as burning coals. He glimpsed a narrow head, pointed triangular ears, a lean, supple body hunched low to the ground.

A cat, Zorro thought. At least six feet long from head to tail, making it about the right size for a mountain lion. But the fur of the mountain lion was a solid tawny color, and Zorro could discern patterns of black spots on its hide even in the forest gloom.

All at once, he realized he was standing eye to eye with a jaguar.

Zorro studied the creature with undiluted wonder, keeping himself absolutely motionless. Though they had occasionally been seen ranging as far north as California, jaguars were far more common in the mountainous jungles of southern Mexico. And what was he to make of its weirdly glowing eyes? As Don Diego, he had traveled extensively in the months after completing his education. During that period he'd had the chance to observe many of the natural world's strange and exotic creatures. Yet those vertical red slits, like tears in the fabric between earth and the infernal depths . . .

There was nothing

The jaguar slunk forward, its uncanny gaze still fixed on Zorro. He tightened his grip on his sword but otherwise remained perfectly still, his own eyes steady on the creature. He was aware—well aware— that any sudden movement on his part might cause it to pounce.

Its padded feet gliding soundlessly over the grass and root clumps, the jaguar came closer, stopped, took two more slow steps. Then it got down on its belly and produced another rasping snarl.

Zorro was able to catch a glimpse of bared white fangs before he again heard the shifting of foliage. Above him, this time.

He snapped his head up and found himself looking at his other inhuman stalker.

Balanced on an overhanging tree limb, the second red-eyed jaguar simultaneously arched its back and lowered its angular head toward the ground. Its claws clicked on dry bark. Zorro saw its tail switching back and forth with excitement, saw muscles winding into tight coils under its fur, saw its hind legs drawing in against its body. Sleek and taut, poised for a deadly jump, the creature was like a living, self-propelled missile . . . one that was about to make Zorro its target.

Aware he had scant hope of avoiding the jaguar's leap, Zorro pulled his sword free of its scabbard in readiness. Leaves spun and fluttered from the trees, sheared off their branches by his darting blade.

Suddenly the jaguar sprang from its perch, letting out a savage roar as it descended. Its great shadow fell over Zorro. He planted his feet apart and braced for the crush of its weight, sweeping his blade upward to drive it into the animal's chest.

But the impact never came—and the reason stunned Zorro more than anything else that had happened to him that night, and possibly more than anything in his experience. For a heartbeat before the jaguar would have completed its downward lunge and impaled itself on his sword point, it vanished.

Simply vanished into thin air.

Zorro blinked, confused. At first he could only suppose it had changed the direction of its leap at the last instant and landed somewhere off to his side. Gripping his sword with both hands, he pivoted on his heel and scanned the area to the immediate left and right. But there was no sign of the creature.

Then he remembered the jaguar that had been following him on the ground and spun around to see whether it was still there, perhaps having been joined by its tree-climbing brother.

It, too, was gone without a trace. Nothing stirred in the brush where it had lurked. As if nothing had been there to begin with.

Behind him, Tornado shuffled a little but was otherwise quiet.

Zorro stood in growing bewilderment. If the jaguars had fled into the darkness, why hadn't he heard them? Stealthy as they were, he couldn't believe such large animals had scrambled off without disturbing so much as a branch. Also, he had been looking straight up at the one that had sprung from the tree. How could he have failed to see it land?

It was, Zorro thought, as if the jaguars hadn't truly existed at all, but rather been hallucinations brought about by the play of shadows and moonlight.

But if he were to believe that . . . what else, then, might be attributed to his imagination?

He slipped back to the edge of the thicket and glanced out toward the Indian camp.

An audible breath escaped his lips. This time the feeling of unreality that washed over him was dizzying.

The laborers were still digging and hauling their burdons under the relentless scrutiny of their guards. And the cloaked man still stood before the stone serpent, watching the camp from high above, his posture full of lordly arrogance.

Only now he was not alone.

Now he was flanked by a pair of huge spotted cats, the two animals heeling beside him like trained pets. And man and beast alike were staring toward the thicket with hellfire-red eyes.

Zorro leaned a hand against a tree trunk. He felt a strange lassitude seeping into his limbs, and was again aware of a malevolent outside force trying to work its way into him—one he neither understood nor was prepared to combat. And part of him knew that to stay where he was much longer was to risk letting it overwhelm him.

Summoning every ounce of willpower, he forced his legs to move toward his horse. He could feel the contained strength in Tornado's frame as he gripped the saddle horn and shakily climbed up onto the leather. Then he swung the horse around and gave the reins an urgent jerk.

Tornado reared and broke into a run, tearing through the underbrush to the wide dirt path, then flying off into the night.

But even as he raced back toward the settled pastures to the south, his cape streaming in the wind, the distance home measured out by the beating of Tornado's hooves, Zorro knew the day would come, and come soon, when he must stand in bitter conflict with the lord of the jaguars.

It was a knowledge that left him cold.

Cold to the bone.

Chapter 7

Insult piled atop outrage! Humiliation added to embarrassment! Laziness and incompetence everywhere
I turn! Your inability to maintain order is trying my
patience, Sergeant!"

Captain Sanches Monastario jabbed a finger at
Garcia from behind his desk, his eyes glaring above
his mustache and chin beard. When those eyes looked
at someone, they always pierced like darts, the sergeant thought. Red-hot, needling darts, hurled suddenly at some soft and vulnerable spot.

He adjusted his bulk in his chair and blinked hard,
not sure how—or even *whether*—to respond. At what
point did words of self-defense sound like excuses?
He'd never been a good judge of that; the line between one and the other seemed so fine as to be un-
discernible. On the other hand, keeping his mouth
shut rarely got him in trouble.

Silence, he decided, was the way to go.

Monastario stared at him another moment, his upper lip trembling with anger. Then he slammed a hand down on his desk twice, hitting it with such force that his quill pen toppled from its holder and went jumping and jittering across the blotter.

"*Madre de dios!*" he snapped. "How long will you continue to sit there like an oversized potato? Your unresponsiveness is maddening!"

Garcia shifted again. Sometimes one simply could not win.

"Commandante, please . . . my men have been doing everything possible to track down this Zorro. You must understand, the mask he hides beneath makes it difficult to know who he is . . . or where to begin searching for him . . ."

"As it was reported to me, several of those men— men whose identities are all too well-known *despite* the disguises they wore—did not have far to look last night, and might have been in a position to capture the scoundrel had they kept their eyes in their heads rather than on a *mestizo* woman's backside."

"I assure you, the incident to which you refer was an aberration. The holiday festivities—"

"—Did not give the King's soldiers freedom to acquit themselves like a pack of drunken louts, staggering about the plaza without their wits. And what of the many acts of thievery they've committed during the past week? Do you also wish to make excuses for them on that account?"

"Commandante, surely you know I would not condone—"

"I know nothing except that news of their behavior must never reach the Viceroy! I refuse to have my reputation tarnished because you are incapable of imposing discipline upon your troops."

Garcia struggled for an appropriate comment, couldn't think of one, and instead produced something between a grunt and a throat-clearing sound—hoping it would satisfy the captain that he was considering their problem, yet was still noncommittal enough to keep his rump out of the frying pan. He certainly wasn't inclined to reveal that he grudgingly admired the Fox for his bold rescue of the girl. Nor was he about to state that he was glad her attackers were locked away in the *calaboso,* regardless of the circumstances that had put them there, or the scandal that might arise because of their status as soldiers. Anyone that went about robbing and harassing defenseless women very much deserved punishment . . . perhaps lancers even more than civilians, since they were expected to set a standard of lawful conduct for the rest of the community.

Of course, he saw why Monastario had reason to be irate. Drunk or not, the men Zorro had bested were trained fighters, and should have made a better accounting of themselves. *Caramba,* the odds had been four to one in their favor!

Garcia watched a fly buzz a rapid, looping course about the room, beating its tiny body against the walls and ceiling as if frantically seeking escape. He found himself sympathizing with its plight. Monastario was regarding him sharply now, leaning so far forward over the desk it almost appeared as if he would lunge for his throat.

The sergeant scratched the perpetual stubble under his fleshy chin, wanting to cringe.

"Listen to my instructions carefully," Monastario

said. "You are to see that those dogs are flogged in public, held in their cells for an appropriate period, and fed nothing but stale bread and water while imprisoned. Also that they are discharged from service immediately after their release. Any pay they are presently due will be withheld as a fine for their reprehensible actions." His mouth curved down in a scowl. "They should be glad I don't send them all to the gallows."

"Indeed," Garcia said sternly, trying to match his tone to Monastario's. "And shall the stolen items found in their barracks be returned to the women they victimized? There is a fair amount of jewelry—earrings, bracelets, necklaces . . ."

Monastario held up a preemptive hand. "And how, may I ask, shall we determine which item belongs to whom?"

Garcia was still scratching under his chin. "Well, we could display them here in the *cuartel* and give people the opportunity to claim them—"

"Are you a total idiot, Garcia? There's nothing like the gleam of gold and silver to bring out the liar in someone. I will not have the women of this pueblo wrestling in the mud over their possession."

"But then what shall we do with them? I—"

"You are to personally bring them here to me. Tonight. Quietly. In plain cloth sacks."

"Yes, but—"

"The jewelry will remain in my safekeeping until such time as we can devise a way to separate the true claims from the false," Monastario continued, ignoring the interruption. His quick eyes leaped to Garcia's face. "This is to stay between the two of us, Sergeant. I do not want a commotion. Understood?"

Garcia looked back at the captain. He was uneasy with the demands being made of him, but recognized that the consequences of disobedience were nothing he wanted to bring down upon his head.

"*Sí,*" he said, puffing out a breath. "I will do as you order, Commandante."

Monastario eyed him for a moment that seemed without end, then finally gave him a satisfied nod.

Garcia suddenly felt that he needed some fresh air.

"Well, the morning awaits, and I'd best be about my duties before it leaves me behind," he said with a nervous little chuckle. He started to heft his weight from the chair. "If I may be excused . . ."

"I wasn't finished. There is another matter to be discussed."

Garcia hesitated, sank heavily back down into the chair.

"You are, I trust, aware of the so-called mission out in the San Fernando valley that has become a beacon to the *peónes.*"

"Of course," Garcia said. "That is, if you mean the settlement of Hidalgo el Cazador."

Monastario nodded, reached for the overturned pen holder, and set it right, outwardly seeming to have calmed . . . although Garcia was not about to make the mistake of thinking his anger had subsided. He had merely packed it down a bit, was all.

"I have heard grumblings about it from the Fransciscan padres at San Luis Rey and San Saba. They call it a place of the devil, and are troubled by my supposed permissiveness in allowing it to stand undisturbed."

Garcia shrugged. "I do not see any harm in such a policy. The poorest Indians go there for food and provisions, and seem happier for whatever guiding influence Don Cazador provides."

"And those who embrace him and remain at the camp cease to tend the fields along the mission circuit. My concern is a pragmatic one . . . and so too, I suspect is that of the priests, despite their pious declarations. The Indians provide us with an essential labor force, and we must not allow it to dwindle. Furthermore, I do not wish to encourage complaints that I am in any way neglecting the missionary effort."

"Commandante, if we forbid the Indians to visit Los Rayos del Sol, or expel Cazador from our territory, we will surely have a revolt on our hands."

"Must you always remind me of the obvious? I know the political realities we face," Monastario said. "I also know that I don't want the long gowns breathing down my neck. They are urging that we take action and we must placate them. This is a delicate situation, sergeant."

"But what can we do?"

"I haven't yet decided." Monastario's features tightened. "For now, however, I am advising you to be ready when the time comes to act . . . and be assured, it will come soon enough."

There was another pause, this one longer than the last. Garcia sat quietly. The fly he had been watching finally located the window and corkscrewed out into the bright light of the still summer morning. He realized that his sympathy for it had turned to something like envy.

Monastario sat back in his chair, his posture unrelaxed and ramrod straight. He clamped his hands together on his desk and studied them, acting as if Garcia was no significance, or had already left the room. It was, Garcia knew, the commandante's usual way of dismissing his subordinates.

Garcia got up as quickly as his voluminous weight allowed, grunting with the effort, the crossbelt he wore over his too-tight uniform tunic—two buttons over his stomach had popped and he hadn't bothered replacing them—stretching outward as if it might snap.

"A pleasant day to you, Commandante," he said, saluting. As he did, the meaty flesh of his upper arms made his sleeves pucker at the seams and strained against the inner curves of his circular, red-and-white epaulettes, warping them oddly out of shape. "I shall keep this discussion firmly in mind and order my men to renew their hunt for Zorro—"

"Enough, Sergeant," Monastario said without looking up at him. "Just leave my sight, for God's sake."

"Certainly, right this mom—"

"Get out now, you brainless, swag-bellied hog!"

Garcia nodded, swallowed, about-faced, and shuffled out the door without another word.

Chapter 8

Sergeant Garcia was sulking in his office, chewing some beef jerky to relieve his distress over Monastario's blunt admonitions—a *hog,* the commandante had called him, as if his girth were the result of some personal weakness, a failure of self-control rather than his zest for life's epicurean pleasures!—when he noticed the clop of hooves on the sun-baked dirt of the plaza outside. Donkey hooves, from the slow, tedious sound of them. They were accompanied by the ear-splitting squeak of dry wood and the irregular *thunk-a-thunk* of wheels that were not quite round, confirming that what approached was a simple *carreta,* the sort of wagon used by peasants who could afford nothing better.

Garcia had thrown open the door to admit the morning breeze while there was still a whiff to speak of; soon enough, the midsummer sun would be beating down on the roof of his office, turning it into a bake-oven. Rocking laboriously forward in his chair now, he peered outside and saw the bulky shadow of the mule-cart move up to his hitch post. A moment later the creaking and thumping stopped and the wagon's rider began to dismount.

Ah well, he thought. The first routine business of the day had arrived . . . his unhappy meeting with the commandante aside. No doubt his visitor would be some fellow with a minor problem or complaint he wished to get off his mind—a dead sheep fouling his well, a dispute with a neighbor over grazing land, perhaps an accusation of a shortage in something or other purchased from a local merchant. Not that Garcia felt he would mind tending to such humdrum affairs. Better to hear the bickering of a dozen irate peasants than to be scolded in needlessly demeaning terms by his superior. And over matters he was powerless to effect! How did Monastario suppose he was to go about exposing Zorro's identity? By questioning every proud *caballero* in Los Angeles who matched the Fox's physical type? Or perhaps insisting that each of them pose for him in a black cloak and half-mask, so that the one who most closely resembled the outlaw might be hauled off to jail as a suspect? There was no reason to cause a public uproar. Despite the awed whisperings that had been uttered about him over the past several months, Zorro was only human. He would trip himself up sooner or later, and in the meantime Garcia preferred not to turn the pueblo inside out.

He gulped down the chunk of jerky he'd been munching and waited for his visitor to enter.

"Olé," he muttered to himself, the sight of the

young woman coming through his doorway making his jaw drop open, and sweeping his troubles with the commandante from his mind like so much dry mud brushed off the tops of his boots.

She was startlingly beautiful, her long, braided hair black as raven feathers, her eyes large and dark, the skin of her high-cheekboned face smooth as silk. Her modest, ankle-length skirt and *reboso* were scarcely enough to hide her curving proportions from any man with two good eyes, a beating heart, and healthy red blood flowing in his veins.

As she stepped through the doorway, Garcia felt his mouth go dry, began to wet his lips, and stopped himself at the last instant, thinking how unseemly it would be to welcome a fair señorita into his office with his tongue hanging out like a thirsty dog's. Still, he was far less able to restrain himself from staring, his eyes wide circles in their puffy nests of flesh . . . and however overpowering he found her loveliness, this time it was not the reason. He had suddenly realized he'd seen her before, and seen her recently, at that— although he did not immediately know *where,* or under what circumstances. Still, he had a feeling it would come to him in a minute.

"*Buenos dias,* Sergeant Garcia," she said in a quiet, reserved voice. "If you have a spare moment, I would speak with you . . ."

"Yes, of course, please come in." His eyes fastened on the girl, Garcia rose clumsily, bumping his knee against the bottom of his desk. He winced from a sharp jolt of pain. "What can I do for y—?"

His mouth dropped open again.

"Is something wrong?" She paused halfway across

the room, looking a little baffled by his queer, slack-jawed expression.

Garcià shook his head and gestured her into a chair in front of his desk. No, nothing was wrong. But he had suddenly realized why the girl looked familiar, and why he'd felt certain the particulars of their earlier meeting would prove worth recalling. Whatever high holiday spirits he had been in two nights past (some of his fellow revelers had tried to convince him he'd been sopped to the gills and staggering in four different directions at once, a ludicrous allegation to be sure), Garcia's senses were never so dull that a pretty señorita would fail to make a lasting impression, and it had struck him that his caller was the very same girl Zorro had rescued from the four costumed knaves in the plaza.

"Might I ask your name, my dear?"

"Arcadia," she replied. "Arcadia Flores. I live some five miles north of the pueblo with my father and brother. You know Alondra Creek?"

"*Sí.*" Garcia sat back down without taking his eyes off her face, almost undershooting his chair in his distraction. Had his rump been any less broad he'd have missed it altogether and crashed heavily to the floor; as it was, the corner of the chair jabbed into a spot where the natural padding was mercifully thick, halting his downward trajectory with only minor discomfort.

"It has good trout fishing," he went on. "There is a small homestead nearby, as I remember."

Arcadia nodded. "That is my family's. We raise some sheep, and I make textiles and garments with their wool to sell at market."

"I believe I saw your weaving on display at the

festival last week." Garcia adjusted his posterior so it would rest more comfortably in his chair. "As a man of refinement and taste, I can attest that you do nice work."

She nodded again, forcing a pale, constricted smile. Then she looked down at her hands and smoothed her skirt over her knees in silence. Garcia waited, rubbing his scruffy face, imagining how soft her cheek would feel against it, how sleek her hair would be under the gliding caress of his palm.

"Sergeant . . ." she said, raising her head. Her gaze met his and he suddenly got the disconcerting sense that she'd caught him in his little fantasy—though, of course, it was a nonsensical thought. Bright and intelligent as they were, the girl's eyes were hardly those of a mindreader.

"Yes?" Garcia asked, hoping he looked sufficiently composed. "Tell me your problem."

She nodded, her features troubled and hesitant. "Do you know of the one they call Hidalgo del Cazador?"

He blinked with surprise. Though framed somewhat differently, the same question had been put to him by the commandante not an hour earlier. Had everyone in town awakened with Cazador's name on their tongues this morning?

She noticed his reaction and regarded him curiously. "Are you certain I've not come at a bad time? If so, I could—"

"No, no. Do not worry yourself. What is it you wish to say about the healer?"

She was still wearing that expression of quiet reserve, but a very different, much harder look seemed to have edged upward beneath its surface.

"Healer," she echoed with unmistakable resentment. "I suppose the term applies. But is it not said that some cures may be worse than the disease?"

"I have heard the phrase, and yet must admit to being confused by its use in this instance," Garcia said. "Most people see Cazador as a good, even a great man . . ."

"If you are speaking of the poor, that is because they are always looking for reasons to believe their lives will get better. He leads them on with hope as if it were a gold nugget at the end of a chain. Let them come within reach, though, and he snatches it away . . . ever making sure it continues to dangle in sight."

"I see," Garcia said, although the truth was that he didn't. In fact, he was no longer merely puzzled, but had altogether lost his grip on what she was talking about. Whether this was because he was too dazzled by her loveliness to keep his mind on what she was saying, or because the words themselves were insufficiently plain, he did not know.

A frown creased his brow. Women, ay-ay! Why did they have to dress everything up in frills and flowers?

"Do you claim that Cazador has stolen something from your family?" he asked. "If that is the case, it seems rather incredible. I mean no offense, but what possession of yours could he possibly want? Everyone knows he is a man of impressive wealth—"

"Sergeant, I beg you to try and understand. He is a thief, yes. But what he steals from people is their *free will.* And he has taken this most precious thing from those I love."

The lines on Garcia's forehead deepened. "How's that, young lady?"

She looked directly into his face, and then, speaking without pause, told him of coming home from the plaza the night before to find her father and brother gone, of Cazador's sudden and terrifying appearance, and finally of the dark promise he had made at the visit's conclusion, omitting any mention of his strange possession of her for fear Garcia would think she'd gone daft . . . and because of her own shame at the feelings that had ignited in her while she'd been in his hypnotic sway.

Garcia listened to her account with growing fascination, his eyes as wide as those of a child being told a scare-story beside a guttering midnight campfire.

"*Madre de dios*, this is quite a tale," he said when she was finished. "I mean, if I were to accept everything you've told me—"

"And why shouldn't you, Sergeant?" she said sharply, her dark eyes lighting with unexpected indignation. "Is it because I am a woman? Or perhaps because a *peón* must never speak of the terrible deeds committed by those of higher birth?"

"There is no call for such testiness," Garcia said. "Being a man of authority here in the pueblo . . . a man of wisdom and insight, most say, though I would not wish to pat my own back . . . I must handle every issue brought before me with prudence. And these charges you make against Don Cazador give me more to think about than most. Never mind the things he is supposed to have said to you. This business about his turning people into mindless slaves . . . it is unbelievable!"

"The truth may often seem that way when it is first

uncovered," she said. Her tone was less harsh now, but the fiery light in her eyes shone as brightly as it had a moment ago, and Garcia thought her anger was not far from taking another flying leap at him. "If you'll only look into what I say—"

"And do that I shall," he said, clearing his throat. "Indeed, a meeting of the town council is scheduled for late next week, and I intend to ask those attending whether they have heard any similar stories about Don Cazador."

"Is that all?" she said. "I tell you my father and brother have been taken away to toil in Cazador's fields like drudge animals, tell you I have been threatened with abduction as well, and the best you can do is promise to address the matter *next week?*"

Garcia spread his hands. What else was was he to do? He certainly could not divulge anything about the Franciscan padres' leeriness toward Los Rayos del Sol. Nor could he mention his precarious position with Monastario, who had explicitly ordered him to adopt a wait-and-see attitude toward Cazador, and stay out of his affairs for the time being. Indeed, if those orders were disobeyed, he might very well find himself in the stockade with the four rogues who had recently accosted the señorita.

"You simply must keep your emotions from getting the better of you," he said. "I see no evidence that Cazador did anything but court you the other night, as any man would to a fair young lady that has caught his eye. No evidence, in fact, that any harm has come to your family members . . . just that they've gone off to do labor for Cazador. *Voluntary* labor, for all we know. And besides, there's nothing wrong with a little hard work—"

He saw the look of unvarnished disgust on her face and broke off his sentence even before she could interrupt him.

"What would you know of work, hard or otherwise?" she exclaimed furiously, springing up from her chair. "You do nothing but sit here on your spreading bottom, while your lancers run about making menaces of themselves."

Garcia flinched. "Mind your tongue, señorita! Such vulgarity from a woman shocks me . . . though perhaps you are not as innocent as you appear!" he said. "For was it not the Fox himself, a known desperado, pressing his lips to your dainty little fingers the other night . . . ?"

She tilted her chin up proudly and took a step toward the desk. "Zorro is a true hero. A champion. Do not sully his name with your foolish tongue."

"Well!" Garcia huffed indignantly, rising himself now. "If you are going to continue this impertinence, I think it would best that you leave."

"Not before you say how you intend to help my family, you thick-headed lout!"

Which, as far as Garcia was concerned, was better than told he had a fat ass. It was also considerably less of an insult than being called a brainless, swag-bellied hog, since it neither made reference to his surplus poundage, nor compared him to a barnyard animal.

Nonetheless, he had to make it clear who was in charge here.

He came around his desk and took hold of Arcadia's right arm, hustling her toward the door.

"Let go of me," she said, unsuccessfully trying to pull away.

"Certainly," Garcia said. He managed to get her as far as the doorway before she stiffened her shoulders, bracing herself against the jamb. "As soon as you learn some manners."

"You would speak of manners while bullying someone half your size? And a *woman,* no less?" she exclaimed vehemently, continuing to resist his efforts to steer her through the door. "How dare you dismiss me so, when it is your job to insure the safety of the people!"

He flushed and tightened his grip on her. The girl was carrying on at quite a volume, and it would not do for anyone out in the plaza to hear him being addressed in such a fashion.

"I do not need anyone to remind me what my job is or isn't, you little shrew—"

Before he could complete his sentence her right hand came up and smacked him full across the face.

Garcia gaped in astonishment, his cheek smarting, his eyes looking as if they would pop from their sockets. Out the corner of his vision he could see men and women watching curiously from scattered points throughout the square . . . exactly the kind of scene he'd wanted to avoid!

"Do you realize you have just struck an officer of the military? Such behavior is impermissible! Impermissible!" he blustered, keenly aware of the gathering crowd's attention. He took a deep breath and lowered his voice a notch, speaking only to Arcadia now, his hand squeezing her arm. "Go on your way before it is too late, señorita. I know you are distressed, and in spite of your foul words and actions, would rather not make an example of you."

"Here is *another* kind of pain to worry about, then!" she cried furiously.

And delivered a swift kick to his right shin.

Garcia released a loud, wounded yelp and hopped backward on his left foot, gripping his opposite ankle with both hands as jagged bolts of lightning shot through it.

The bray of jeering laughter he heard from the crowd was the last straw.

"You, woman, are under arrest!" the sergeant shouted. Still bouncing up and down on one leg, he jerked his head toward a pair of lancers who had been drawn from across the plaza by the disturbance . . . and devil take him if there weren't *grins* on their faces. What had he done to deserve such a wretched start to the day?

"Behind bars with her until she learns how to be civil!" Garcia bellowed. He jabbed a finger at the lancers as they approached, noting that both were looking at the ground to hide their amusement. "And stop smirking or I'll discipline the two of you as well! I've had enough disrespect for one morning! *Enough,* I say!"

Nursing his leg, he watched the uniformed men bracket Arcadia—one taking hold of each arm—and conduct her past him to the short hallway behind his office.

"Shame on you, Sergeant Garcia." Her eyes flinging needles of disdain, Arcadia glared over her shoulder at him as she was lead away. "You are nothing but a disgrace to your uniform!"

A moment later she vanished into the holding area behind his office. The sergeant heard the jangle of keys, the grate of rusty hinges, and then the heavy clang of a cell door slamming shut.

His face beet red, Garcia looked at the staring faces outside the doorway and frowned. Was that accusation he detected in their expressions? What was going on here? He'd been completely justified in locking up the girl . . . hadn't he?

He stood there immobilized by embarrassment and confusion, his eyes sweeping the crowd. None of them were laughing anymore. And over by the market stalls across the plaza . . . that old man watching him and shaking his head . . . the one with the wild, billowing cloud of grey hair . . . wasn't he a servant for the de la Vega family? Were even the pueblo's common *domestics* now passing judgement upon him?

Bah! What did the deaf-mute know? Or anyone who hadn't heard the entire argument, for that matter? True, the girl had been under distress. But to speak to him as she had, to call him a do-nothing and ridicule his anatomy . . .

Garcia grunted in dismay and turned his back on the whole lot of them, the hot sting of her words somehow worse than the physical pain of her kick.

Standing near his wagon in front of the trading post, Bernardo saw Garcia limp back into his office, then bash his door shut behind him. He sighed and heaved a sack of feed into the flatbed, still shaking his head with sadness and disapproval. Asinine as Garcia could be, the sergeant had never struck him as the type who would lock up an obviously distraught woman.

Well, he thought, one never knew, which was why it was always good to keep one's eyes and ears open.

He had ridden into town for supplies and, as usual, had simultaneously found himself getting hold of important information.

It was information he wanted Diego to hear about as soon as possible.

Chapter 9

Muttering a silent prayer, Private Esteban Díaz shook the dice cup resolutely in both hands, confident the Lady of Good Fortune would finally grace him with her blessing, and help him win back some of the gold coins he'd lost to the pot that night. Of course, he'd been equally confident before his preceding rolls, and they had done nothing but get him into deeper and deeper hock . . . but it was best not to jinx himself with such thoughts.

He glanced about the room and noted the impatient looks being flung at him from his fellow players. Though only Esteban and two others were officially assigned to the prison detail, all five wore the dark blue uniforms of men-at-arms. The jailhouse was as good a place as any for serious gambling; better, in some ways, than the cantina or barracks, with their constant, distracting hubbub. Of course, he doubted

Garcia or Monastario would be pleased to see their lancers gulping tequila from the huge ceramic *olla* making the rounds between them, especially with four prisoners—*five* counting the woman Garcia had arrested that morning—presently in their charge. But they weren't going anywhere, and while the cats were away . . .

"*Hola, mis amigos*—"

This from the larger of the two cells on Esteban's left—specifically the one holding the soldiers that had run amok the other night, while disguised as holiday revelers. In fact, they were still wearing the idiotic costumes they had donned before committing their string of misdeeds, that churlish behavior having cost them the right to proper military attire . . . in addition to the even harsher penalities it had brought upon their heads.

"Quiet, we're busy," Esteban replied without any pause in his dice-rattling. He'd recognized the voice that had called out as belonging to Miguel, the idiot in the angel's garb, and didn't wish to be plagued with his foolery at the moment. Ah yes, his palms were itching, a premonition that an even thirty-six was on the way . . . or was an itching *nose* supposed to be the lucky sign? "And don't call us your friends."

"But you and I have always been the *best* of friends! Why just last week, Esteban . . ."

"Nor do any of us wish to have your foul tongue sully our names. As a respectable member of the military, and one of those chosen to guard you until the whip licks your bones clean of flesh tomorrow morn, I prefer that you address me as *Señor Soldado*."

"Whatever, *muchacho*—"

"I said to call me—"

"Mr. Soldier, I mean," Miguel said. "My point is that a week ago, when we were bunkmates rather than jailer and captive, you promised to introduce me to your sister when she comes up to visit from Durango . . ."

"Hah, stop with the lies! Never in a million years would I speak of her in the presence of such a worm as you—"

"Elena! You told me her name is Elena, that you used to watch her bathe in secret, and that she has a body like a—"

"That is enough! For one thing, if I *did* mention her at all, it was before I learned you were the most dastardly of thieves, hiding behind the mask of a holy saint, no less! And for another, there is a lady present—an intended *victim* of yours, I might add—whom I would spare from your vulgar remarks . . ."

"I was merely going to repeat *your* choice comments," Miguel said in a chiding tone. "Besides, the so-called lady to whom you refer is nothing but a slatternly *mestizo,* locked up for striking Garcia in full view of—"

"*Enough,* I said!"

"Let's get on with the game," said one of the other guards, a man whose hulking size and mean disposition had earned him the nickname of *Bajista*—Bear. "Either throw the dice or pass 'em, Esteban."

"I second that," said Pedro, yet another of the soldiers on duty. He swigged tequila from the jug, blinking twice as it poured down his throat like liquid fire. "I'm eager for you to lose some more money."

"Why are you talking to *me*?" Esteban said. "You want to complain, do it to the caged animal who's been ruining my concentration."

Bajista scowled.

"Quit making excuses and throw," he said.

Esteban considered just handing the dice over to Bajista and telling him where he could shove them, cup and all, but then caught the glaring look in his eyes and decided to keep his peace.

He gave the cup a final shake, blew a good luck kiss over it, and cast the dice.

They tumbled across the packed dirt floor, coming to rest against the far corner of the room.

Crossing the middle and index fingers of both hands, Esteban jumped over to them and stood adding up his points. He'd rolled a two, a six, a five, another six . . .

Guffaws from all sides.

Esteban didn't need to finish his count to know he'd gone bust. He not only felt his stomach sink, but found himself wishing the rest of him would drop down with it until he fell out of sight through a hole in the earth.

"Too bad, Mister Loser," Miguel shouted between hiccups of laughter.

"Best pay up before your *compañeros* toss you behind lock and key with us," one of his cellmates chimed in.

"If they do, he'd better stay awake 'round the clock," said another of the prisoners, a man named Jorge who had been wearing the Death's Head mask when apprehended. "We don't like his kind around here."

"Keep your uncivilized mouths shut or I'll shut them for good." Esteban snatched the *olla* away from the man standing beside him and slugged back some tequila. "That goes especially for you, Miguel."

"*Me?* It is Jorge who threatened you . . ."

"And it is you who *instigated* him."

Miguel looked pained. "But—"

"Are we going to shoot the dice or spend the entire night bickering with these felons?" said Pedro. He had leaned back against the wall, extracted a tobacco pouch from his tunic, and begun rolling a smoke. "The chatter's getting on my nerves."

"Allow me into the game and I'll be glad to stop talking," said Miguel. "One round with you is all I ask, Esteban. I can throw the dice just as well from behind these bars as outside them."

Now it was Esteban who blurted jeering laughter. "And what do you intend to *wager,* dog? I happen to know the commandante has ordered that your full pay be garnished."

Miguel eyed him steadily.

"True, I've no money to put up, but there are other types of bets that can be made," he said with a cryptic smile.

Esteban shook his head . . . but had to admit to being a little curious. Still holding the jug, he went across the room and stood directly in front of the big cell.

"Such as . . . ?"

"If I lose, I will get on my knees and kiss your bare bottom."

"And should chance turn the other way?" Esteban took another long swallow of liquor. "I must tell you, Miguel, I am tempted . . . but have no desire to put my lips to your filthy rear under any circumstances."

"Nor would you have to." Miguel said. Grinning shiftily, he cocked his head toward the cell beside him, where Arcadia sat on the hard flat of wood that passed for a cot. "Winning gets me a few minutes alone with the señorita."

Until this point Arcadia had stood pressed against the bars of her cell, silently listening to the crude exchanges between her guards, thinking herself forgotten amid their preoccupation with the dice game. Call it ignorance or innocence, she had failed to anticipate the combustive passions ignited by the mixture of drinking and gambling, and felt she should have known better.

She looked out at Esteban, her eyes wide circles of dismay. He had snapped laughter at Miguel's suggestion . . . but had not walked away from his cell, and Arcadia feared that was the more telling indication of what was going on in his intoxicated brain.

"Are you *mad*? If Garcia should hear about it . . ."

"A kiss would satisfy me . . . which is to say I would do nothing to spoil her questionable virtue," Miguel said. "Mind you, I only want a brief, pleasant memory to divert me as I stand lashed to the whipping post tomorrow."

Esteban was still looking at his prisoner with curiosity . . . and now Arcadia could see something else in his expression as well, a sort of base temptation that made her heart sink. Without even being conscious of her movements, she backed away from the cell door and cowered against the wall.

"Your lips to *all* our backsides if you lose," he said at length. "That's the bet, or nothing!"

Miguel thrust his hand through the bars of his cell.

"You've got it! Ah yes, you do!" he exclaimed, cackling.

Esteban turned toward Arcadia's cell and hesitated, weighing the consequences of his actions if they were

ever revealed to Garcia. How had he allowed Miguel
to tweak him so? But things had gone too far along
for him to even consider backing down. For how
could he have second thoughts about his own prop-
osition without looking ridiculous?

"The dice!" Miguel urged. He turned up his palm,
spread his fingers, and wriggled them covetously. "Put
'em here!"

Esteban regarded Arcadia another moment, then
tore his eyes from her despondent face and went to
retrieve the dice.

In the rectangle of shadows behind the jailhouse, the
blotted figures of a horse and rider came to a halt
under the building's red tile eaves. They had made
slow progress since entering the plaza . . . but stealth
and watchfulness took precedence over haste, at least
at this stage of things, thought the man in the saddle.
And speed would be of the essence soon enough,
would it not?

His reins loose in his black-gloved fingers, the rider
glanced about alertly, his eyes making careful sweeps
of the yard, probing its darkest corners through the
oval slits of a bandit's mask.

For the moment, no one was in sight.

He slid an affectionate hand over his mount's long,
supple neck and leaned forward a little to give it a
hushed command. The stallion obediently moved
closer to the rear wall of the jailhouse and then
stopped again.

Now the man slid his feet from the stirrups, put his
hands over the pommel of his saddle, and boosted
himself to a standing position atop the horse's back,
briefly extending his arms for balance. The horse re-

leased a whiffling breath but did not shift an inch.

Less than three seconds later, the rider craned his head back to study the edge of the rooftop, steadier on his feet, a languid crawl of breeze swishing the bottom of his cloak over the tops of his boots.

"My apologies for using you as a stepladder, Tornado," he said in a whispered undertone. "Your kind disposition is not taken for granted, I promise."

His right hand slipped under his flowing cloak, reappeared grasping the silver-gilt haft of a bullwhip. Still eyeing the rooftop, he raised the whip to shoulder height and flicked it out with a loose, easy movement that was part toss of the arm, part snap of the wrist, and entirely seamless in its execution.

The length of plaited leather sang through the air and wrapped around the jailhouse's narrow smokestack.

Pleased by his aim, the man jerked down hard on the whip to test it and concluded that it had looped fast around the anchoring chimney. Then, both hands clenched around the whip's haft, he launched off the saddle, swinging forward as he did so. The soles of his boots touched against the sunbleached walls with only the faintest of scuffing sounds.

He scaled the wall like a bobcat climbing a tree and scrambled up onto the roof.

Once on top, he wound the bullwhip into a neat coil again and paused briefly to fetch in a breath, surveying the plaza from his new vantage.

As expected, it remained quiet and deserted.

Assuming low crouch, he moved lightly over the tiles to the opposite end of the roof, lowered himself to his belly, and peered over the edge. Yellow lamplight spilled from a window perhaps ten feet below him. And something else . . . overlapping male voices, coarse grunts of laughter.

It seems the guards are having a grand old time tonight, the masked man thought. *I wonder if they'll thank me for seeing that their party's a memorable one, filled with light and dazzlement.*

He pulled his head back from the lip of he roof, unstrapped the large, black leather shoulder-pouch he had been carrying, and moved the bone slide along the drawstring to open it.

A moment later Zorro began emptying its contents onto the rooftop.

The six hand-thrown missiles, or *grenades*, that he'd brought from the cave had been devised from linen packets filled with gunpowder and magnesium and then secured to wooden handles with rawhide bands. Just to make things more colorful, Bernardo had, in his inventive wizardry, added a further chemical ingredient to each before tying it shut—a sprinkle of potassium chloride in one, a pinch of copper nitrate in another, some strontium nitrate in a third, and so forth. Running from the packets were simple fuses fashioned by dipping one-inch twists of paper into a solution of water, granulated lead and saltpeter, then leaving them to dry in the hot afternoon sun.

To ignite the fuses, Zorro had brought along a flintlock pistol secretly borrowed from his father's collection, and a tin flask of lamp oil with a wick projecting from its cap. He had once seen an expert in the ways of wilderness survival use a flintlock to start a flame by plugging the touchhole, and then loading the pan with tinder instead of gunpowder. He very much hoped to duplicate that trick tonight. Now he fished the loaded pistol and flask out of his pouch, set the flask down on the roof tiles beside the grenades, cocked the hammer, and squeezed the trigger. There was an orange flash as sparks went shooting into the tinder. Then a curl of smoke, and the sweet odor of burning bark.

Olé! he thought.

With the pistol in his right hand, Zorro raised the flask with the other and placed the wick against the smoldering material in the frizzen, blowing gently on both to kindle the fire. A few seconds later the wick caught, and then flared into a bright orange teardrop of flame, burning steadily, its bottom end soaking up fuel from the flask

Zorro smiled thinly. The preliminaries had worked magnificently, but it remained to be seen whether his overall performance would meet with equal success.

He heard more rough laughter from below and quickly reached for one of the grenades, not wanting to waste another second.

"I won you on the fair and square, Esteban!" Miguel hooted from his cell, gesticulating at the dice he had just thrown. "Thirty-six to your twenty-two! Now quit mourning your loss and fetch the key to the lady's *boudoir*."

Esteban looked at the dice, fuming. The filthy crab louse had rolled the very number for which he'd been praying all night.

It suddenly struck him that their wager might have been one of the worst ideas he'd ever had.

"You mind how far you go with her," he said, and reluctantly pulled the key ring off its wall peg. "You'll be allowed nothing more than what we agreed upon."

Miguel stuck out his tongue and made a slurping

sound, then smacked the air with loud, vulgar kisses. "Don't sour my victory with needless warnings. My lips await their soulful treat!"

There was laughter from the soldiers and other prisoners. Bajista guzzled from the *olla* and hiccuped.

Cowering in her cell, Arcadia raised a hand to just below her neck and clutched the collar of her dress in an unconscious defensive gesture. She heard the jangle of keys as Esteban found the one to his prisoner's cell, then watched him unlock its door and then swing it open, motioning Miguel out into the office.

Miguel turned toward her cell, still wiggling his tongue and burlesquing kisses.

"Don't do it," she said, not addressing him at all, but instead looking past him at the man who was ostensibly his guard. "If your superiors learn of this—"

"A bet's a bet, señorita, even with a lowly creature such as this," he said, nodding his head toward Miguel. "And a kiss is only a kiss, after all. Shut your eyes and it'll be over and done before you know it; I'll make sure you have extra water to wash away the taste."

She shook her head in disgust and clamped her jaw tightly, fighting back a rush of tears. No matter what, she promised herself, she would not give her tormentor the pleasure of seeing her cry.

No matter what.

Esteban moved up to her cell door, put the key into the lockplate, and turned it.

The door opened, and Miguel stepped forward, leering with degenerate glee, his arms outstretched as he went to embrace her.

That was when the first explosion went off outside

the jailhouse, a blinding emerald-green starburst of light that stopped him dead in his tracks, and threw everyone around her into confusion.

Zorro had raised the curtain on his little spectacle. A heartbeat after he hurled the diversionary grenade from his perch atop the roof, splashing the night with green brilliance, Zorro lit another one and sent it flying in a different direction. He watched it tumble toward the ground, its fuse sizzling, then shielded his eyes as a glaring scarlet fireball erupted to the right of the jailhouse, flinging off showery fountains of sparks.

He held his improvised lighter to another grenade, wound up for a throw as its fuse hissed down to a sparkling nub, pitched it over the opposite side of the roof, and then tossed the remaining fireworks in rapid succession, turning the plaza into a demon's bowl of multicolored flame. The night throbbed and swirled with bangs and flashes. Streaks of violet scribbled across the darkness. Brimstone-yellow clouds floated in the air like glowing, smoky wraiths. Pink, blue, and white pinwheels zipped past each other in crazily looping trajectories. Rose-red blossoms expanded with convulsive force, hung briefly above the plaza, and then dispersed, breaking apart into scattered, shimmering petals.

Zorro had barely released his final grenade when the jailhouse door slammed open and nearly a half dozen men came rushing out into the plaza, all of them wearing the blue uniforms and crossbands of King's lancers, all shouting in bewilderment, and all about to have the biggest surprise of the night literally drop down on their heads.

*   *   *

"Who is out here?" Esteban screamed as he emerged from the building. In his confusion, he had not only forgotten Arcadia and Miguel, but the fact he'd left both their cells wide open.

"This is *madness!*" Bajista growled at his heels.

"*Ay,* the sky is on fire!" Pedro shrieked, bumping up behind them. He blinked at an eye-watering pop of orange-red brightness, a fearful, baffled expression on his face. "What have we done to provoke the wrath of Heaven?"

"My advice would be to worry about that when you reach the hereafter, toy soldiers," a voice said from above. "For it is *my* anger that is your immediate problem!"

Pedro was the first to look up and see what appeared to be a living shadow bound from the ledge of the roof, a great black cape rippling around his shoulders, his sword a wicked flicker of silver in his hand.

"*Un espectro!*" Pedro let out, his eyes wide, his lips stretched over his teeth in a grimace of utter panic.

The other two lancers whirled toward the jailhouse at his horrified shout, their eyes shooting upward toward the descending figure. Pyrotechnic light splashed their features with garish color, momentarily giving them the appearance of dazed, befuddled clowns in peculiar makeup.

Reacting a beat ahead of the others, Bajista reached for his own sword, certain the black-clad demon was about to alight on top of them—but even as the weapon left its scabbard their attacker executed an aerial flip that abruptly changed the direction of his plunge, bringing him down *behind* the three stunned lancers.

"Where *is* he, Bajistia?" Esteban cried at the top of his lungs. "What does he want from us?"

Zorro showed him.

The lancers had scant gone racing outside when Arcadia realized she had been left unguarded . . . which did not, unfortunately, mean she was alone.

She looked at the man in front of her, read the single-minded intent in his expression, and drew in a steadying breath. Before she could even think of escaping her cage, she would have to find some way to escape the vicious beast who had been let *into* it.

"Now we settle accounts for the trouble you've caused me, señorita," Miguel said. He was standing in the doorway of the cell, his hands reaching for her, his eyes gleaming with a base, sordid kind of malice. "Sure of yourself, you were, the other night. Striking a pretty pose for El Zorro, letting him plant gentlemanly kisses on the back of your exquisite hand. Well, he isn't here to protect you, and I'm no gentleman."

He came closer.

"Don't be a fool," she said, fighting to keep an even tone. "You have a chance to get away. Do it while you can. I've done nothing to you."

He snorted laughter and continued to advance. "Nothing, little temptress? If it hadn't been for you, I'd be looking forward to morning roll call at the *cuartel,* not a public flogging."

She stepped backward, suddenly felt the edge of her cot pressing against her legs, and knew she could retreat no further.

"I tell you again, you're making a mistake not to flee," she said, trying one last appeal. "They cannot put you to the whip if you are gone from here—"

"Gone? Gone *where*? Into the desert? Burrowed down in a hole with rodents, snakes, and scorpions?" His face knotted into a vengeful sneer. "No, I'll take my medicine rather than become a fugitive, thanks."

Arcadia saw then that his anger had made him completely irrational, and braced herself for his attack.

It came with a bullish, headlong charge that would have hurled her bodily to the floor of the cell had she not been prepared. As it was, she surprised her attacker by springing aside in the bare nick of time.

Unable to halt his furious momentum, he went rushing past her shoulder and straight into the thick wooden board that passed for a sleeping cot, then launched clear over it and collided with the wall.

He hit with a loud smack of flesh and bone, rolled backward over the cot, and crashed to the floor in a howling rage, a large, streaming gash on his forehead.

Arcadia started past him, desperate to reach the cell door before he could scramble to his feet—and had come within an inch of it when she felt a hand clamp around her ankle and pull her savagely off balance.

She fell hard, her legs flying out from under her, the air whoofing from her mouth as her side struck the floor.

"You're faster than I bargained for, neighbor, but not fast enough!" Miguel screamed, belting out wounded laughter. He lifted himself to his knees and glared down at her, blood pouring over his brow. "*Now* let's see you refuse my affections!"

The soldiers went scrambling as Zorro flew into their midst, his whirlwind speed having taken them by surprise.

Esteban thrust out his sword in what Zorro's fencing instructor in Madrid would have called a *prime* position—albeit a sloppy and blundering one—but Zorro parried effortlessly, crossing blades, sending him reeling into one of the other soldiers. Both man crashed to the dirt in a tangled pile of arms and legs.

Zorro spun to his left, saw Pedro charging in with his own weapon drawn, and ducked below the glittering horizontal arc of his weapon as it swept across his chest, going down into a full crouch. Pedro looked about in confusion, his head rotating from side to side as if he were trying to decide where his opponent might have gone, and had no sooner dropped his gaze toward the ground when Zorro sprang up well inside his reach, knocking Pedro's sword from his hand with a blow to his inner forearm, then snapping his foot out in a kick to Pedro's middle.

The soldier doubled over gasping, his blade twirling free of his grip. Zorro kicked the sword away before he could recover it and pushed him back hard with both hands, bowling him into the hitching rail in front of the *calaboso*. Wood cracked and snapped in a blizzard of splinters as he caromed through the railposts, his arms flapping like ineffectual wings. He thudded to the ground perhaps a yard from his toppled fellows, the back of his head slamming against a wall to knock the consciousness out of him.

Zorro took a quick breath, whisked his eyes in a partial circle. He had counted five soldiers altogether pouring out the jailhouse door, and, looking off to his right now, saw one of the remaining two taking flight, scooting across the plaza like a terrified rabbit. Which left the big man, the one who'd been called Bajista—

He had no sooner realized that Bajista must have

dropped back around the corner of the jailhouse than the soldier charged him from the rear, roaring like a jungle animal, his heavy boots pounding the dirt, moving with a swiftness that seemed impossible for someone his size.

Zorro started to whirl out of the way, but his reaction was a hair too slow. All at once a brawny forearm hooked around his throat and clamped off his windpipe, another arm locking across his chest like a metal bar, bending him backward . . .

Threatening to crush the very life out of his body.

As she fell on her shoulder with jarring impact, Arcadia snapped her head away from the man shuffling toward her, her cheek pressing against the floor, her eyes leaping to something they'd glimpsed a split-second earlier, an object resting several feet from where she lay.

The key ring.

Esteban must have dropped it, let go of it in his distraction, lost the keys when he'd gone running outside to investigate the explosions.

She groped for it frantically, extending her fingers until they trembled from the effort.

"Ain't you a lively one!" Miguel exclaimed, crazed with anger, his face hovering less than an inch above her own. He had shuffled toward her on hands and knees and she could feel his moist breath gusting against her cheeks. Blood oozed from the cut on his forehead, tracking down over his left eye, his nose and mouth. He shook it off like a hound shaking water from its coat, sweaty locks of hair slapping his cheeks, spattering crimson droplets down on Arcadia.

"*Ain't you a handful indeed!*" he shouted, then

puckered his blood-smeared lips and bent still closer to her.

Reaching, reaching, her fingernails scraping over the floor, her arm feeling as if it would tear from its socket, Arcadia at last snatched the key ring into her grasp. Gripping one of the skeleton keys by its handle, she jabbed its bit up into her assailant's face, up into the raw, parted flesh of his wound, up and up until its metal teeth were buried deep inside it . . . and then gave it a sharp, sudden twist.

Miguel screamed and clapped his hands over his face, rolling away from her, kicking and flailing on the floor like a man in the throes of an uncontrollable seizure.

Overtaken by a fearful urgency, dreading what would happen if Miguel's agonized contortions subsided before she fled his presence, Arcadia gathered her legs underneath her and lunged for the door.

Gasping for air, Zorro fought without success to escape Bajista's hold. Bajista tightened it, tightened it, lifting him up off the ground, arching him backward until his spine was in danger of snapping like a branch bent past its tolerance. Zorro could feel the air being squeezed from his throat and lungs, feel his strength failing, feel his sword beginning to slip from his fingers. Unless he acted quickly and decisively he was finished.

Pain wailing through his back and ribcage, Zorro jammed his left elbow back into his opponent's chest once, twice, a third time, a fourth.

Bajista's clench weakened perceptibly but did not break.

His lungs aching, black motes wheeling across his

vision, Zorro hit him over and over again, barraging his chest with elbow slams. Finally the arms around his body loosened—just a little, just enough. Dragging in a breath, Zorro slipped free of Bajista's grasp, pivoting to face him as his bootheels met the ground, simultaneously feinting to the left with his blade.

Though still rocked by Zorro's blows, Bajista had nonetheless retained enough of his senses to see the sword point coming at him from that direction. He shifted to the right to avoid it . . . and inadvertently placed his chin in the path of Zorro's driving fist.

Before the soldier could recover, Zorro snapped off a series of quick jabs to his face, bobbed under a misaimed counterpunch, and caught him with an uppercut that took all the strength out of his legs. His eyes glazing, Bajista lurched drunkenly forward, his meaty hands balled into fists . . .

And was knocked on his face as Zorro sprang lightly aside, throwing a foot across his path to trip him.

Giving his huge, immobile form a hurried glance, Zorro turned toward the jailhouse—and to his near-complete surprise saw Arcadia come racing out of the door as if the devil himself were at her heels.

He dashed over to her, his cape billowing out behind him, and had to stop her from falling to the ground as she propelled herself into his arms.

"Zorro!" She clutched his shoulders, her chest hitching against him, her long hair spilling into her eyes. "I . . . those men, they—"

"Later, señorita," he said. "We've both had enough excitement for one evening, I think . . . and had best quit the scene before reinforcements arrive."

Without awaiting a response, he took her hand and

led her around behind the jailhouse. Tornado whiffled happily when he saw his master approach, his tail brushing back and forth, his dark eyes showing a relief that seemed almost human in its warmth and intensity.

Zorro helped Arcadia mount up sidesaddle, then swung atop the horse behind her and slid his arms around her sides to grip the reins.

"Are you steady enough?" he asked.

She nodded wordlessly, her back to his chest.

A high-spirited grin spread across Zorro's face.

"Into the night, Tornado!" he cried. "And give it your best!"

His mane tossing, his hooves hammering the ground, the stallion did just that, vaulting forward like a black bolt of lightning, and quickly leaving the pueblo far behind.

Chapter 10

The glory of the Los Angeles sunrise touched Arcadia Flores in that precious, sweet moment between sleep and awakening. It was the time of magic, when a bridge could be built between dreams and awareness, when fantasies could escape to a netherworld that was not quite flesh and not quite fog.

She stretched in that moment of warmth and light, savoring the feel of the expensive linen, the deep, padded cushioning of the overstuffed mattress, and the soft richness of the pillow beneath her head. It was luxury she had never known, but had always wanted to experience. It was a sense of wealth she had always secretly desired and somehow felt she deserved.

Didn't all young women wish to be princesses? To suddenly be discovered to be descended from royalty? To be whisked away to a palace, covered in glorious gowns, showered with gems, and worshipped as an eternal beauty? These were dreams to be discarded with the day, to be replaced with hard work and honest love of one's family, but in this realm between rest and survival, what harm would one fantasy do?

For a moment, Arcadia forgot herself and the trauma she had suffered these past few nightmarish days. She was not the struggling seamstress leered at for her beauty and then looked down upon for her lowly station. She was the consort and companion of the mysterious renegade known as El Zorro.

By night, she imagined, she rode with him in black silks, giving him the passion he needed to continue his quest: to free the peoples of Los Angeles and all California from the iron yoke of oppression and corruption. But by day she was his humble wife, a compassionate partner who cooked his meals, cleaned his home, tended his needs, and rested with him in preparation for the battles the darkness would bring.

Their lives were pure and powerful. Their secrets were as deep as their caring for their people and one another. Given all the danger they shared, their time of comfort was short but of vital importance. So the time they shared together had to be quiet and special. She reached for him now—her savior, her solace, her secret. The man they called "the fox." The man she called . . .

"Don Diego?" Her voice seemed unnatural, distant, as if coming from another person. She blinked, realizing the image that she saw was not a man at all. It was a portrait . . . not of the useless young scholar the old women of the village clucked about, but the vital adolescent who had left for the University of Madrid so long ago.

Arcadia blinked again, and the swirling colors of

the young man's face came into focus, as did the people around him. It was an image out of time, streaked with the brush strokes of memory. Arcadia felt a strange rush of excitement in the back of her mind, dimly recalling her feelings as a young girl whenever she would catch a glimpse of this young man playing games with his laughing friends or riding with his family.

He was so full of life, that one, smiling with open affection, but always so intent on doing his best— whether it was kicking a shuttlecock into a tiny net during the plaza festivals or tending the horses in his father's stables. Arcadia felt a pang of regret. If only he had not channeled his abilities into book knowledge and letters . . . if only had studied the arts of fighting and science. Perhaps then he would have been of some help in this time of trouble. Perhaps then he would have been more like the masked avenger the people called El Zorro. . . .

All these thoughts were swept from her mind as she saw the face of the woman seated beside Diego de la Vega. It was his mother, the wife of Don Alejandro. She had an inner beauty which put Arcadia's to shame. It was a strength she fervently wished she possessed. It was a serenity in the face of tragedy she prayed she, too, could someday call upon.

Tears burned in the corner of Arcadia's eyes, feeling only sorrow for the men this extraordinary woman left behind. It was she, not Arcadia, who was truly fit to be a mate for a hero as grand as The Fox. She would not have cried alone in her bed every night, begging for her father and brother to return. She would not have nearly fallen victim to her family's captor. She would have not so foolishly shamed the local constable, no matter how impotent and farcical he appeared. And she would not have been left at the mercy of a lustful scoundrel who had trapped Arcadia so ignominiously on the dirt floor of the local dungeon . . .

The glorious sunlight dried her tears as Arcadia slowly blinked the sleep from her eyes. She realized she was staring at a painting which hung on the side wall of a handsomely appointed room. The sumptuous bedclothes were not a dream, nor was the most comfortable nightgown she had ever worn. Her eyes moved to stare down at the detailed brocade that lined the bodice of the evening dress, which rippled across her like refreshing spring air with every movement.

Arcadia Flores sat up in the heavy, wooden, four-poster bed, shocked into total awareness. Memories exploded in her addled mind like crashing surf. The stink of the prison floor, the stench of the man pinning her, the feel of the steel key sinking into muscle, and then tearing into unyielding flesh . . . !

Arcadia gripped her face with a shuddering moan, and then the memories raced to the renegade in black. The masked man who caught her in her terrified flight, led her out of her pueblo prison, and embraced her aboard the saddle of his magnificent steed. And then she remembered the wind in her face, the twinkling stars above them, and the night which seemed to close in upon her like enveloping hands.

"Señorita Flores?" The words seemed to come from both inside and outside her head. They began in the lyrical tones of a woman the concerned maternal tones of the de la Vega mother and wife. But they ended in the whispered call of the son. The ineffectual sage named Diego.

Arcadia looked beyond the end of the bed, where the wood, stone, metal, and adobe of the walls encircled two doors made of glass. Pale white curtains fluttered on either side of these glass doors, which were opened inward. Through them she could just barely make out a figure beyond. Almost as if she were still not in control of her own will, Arcadia pulled back the luxurious bed covers and her feet sought the cool stone of the floor.

She marveled at the softness and comfort of the gown, which would not have been out of place at a breakfast or even luncheon table. Once she stood, its flowing hem covered even her feet. Only its deep u-shaped bodice might be considered immodest, but only by the plaza's eldest citizens, though even they would have to admire its intricate and delicate beadwork.

She stood for a moment, regaining her balance and waiting for a moment of dizziness to pass. It was only then that the full weight of the past days' agony came to her. She put a hand on the baseboard of the four-poster to steady herself, then took a first, tenuous step toward the rippling curtains and open glass doors.

"Zorro?" she tried to say, but the sound emerged as a small, fallen bird's cry.

She found herself standing in the open doorway, stunned silent by the view. The glory that was the county of the angels rolled and swooped out before her, its opulent colors of brown and green and tan and blue filling her eyes and soul.

"Señorita Flores?" the voice said again—this time unmistakably that of the man she knew as Diego de la Vega. She turned to see him, haloed by the intense, early-morning Los Angeles light—a haze that rendered his outline indistinct. But there was more to it than that. There was something different about him; cathartically different.

Arcadia stared at his kindly, gentle, solicitously smiling face, trying to decide what was wrong. Still weak from her ordeal, a strange, errant thought slipped easily into her mind. It was a thought she might never have had otherwise, but it was now one that came to her with the weight of truth. It was as if the flesh of Don Diego's face had been replaced by soft, pale, cunningly forged steel.

"Señorita Flores," he said a third time. "I am ashamed . . ."

Arcadia blinked rapidly, realizing that he was not the man she admired or the one who had saved her, yet she stood with him on a small balcony as if they were man and wife the night after a sacred marriage. Still, she did not flee nor cover the skin of her throat with the material of the billowing curtain. She felt the strength of the de la Vega wife and mother flow into her.

"There is no need," she tried to say, although it came out in a whisper. "You have given me the sanctuary of your home to keep me safe and protected . . ."

"No," said the man, still smiling sympathetically at her. "You do not understand. I did not rescue you to save you."

Arcadia blinked again—the blazing sun, bright colors, and puissant haze forcing her to narrow her eyes. "You?" she said faintly. "But . . ."

"I rescued you for my own purposes," Diego de la

Vega said distantly, looking out to the new land his mother had loved so much. "I rescued you because I was frightened by my own weakness. I rescued you because I wanted to feel strong . . . yet, even so, I was still nearly killed by a sole member of the ineffectual lancers. . . ."

His jaw tightened, and then he looked back with a mix of emotions that made Arcadia move back a step.

"And you," he said with shame. "You were nearly . . . had you not saved yourself . . . !"

Arcadia gripped the side of the door to keep upright. She was so cursedly weak . . . yet this man, a man who should have been strong for her, a man who should be leading his people in rebellion . . . this man was apologizing like a chastised schoolboy for things he had not done . . . things he would never do. There wasn't time for this. There was no time!

"Don Diego," she beseeched him. "Where is the one man who actually rescued me. Where is the man they call El Zorro?"

"El Zorro?" he echoed bitterly. "There is no Zorro . . . Zorro is dead."

The words seemed to echo inside Arcadia's head. Even as she heard them she knew it was not true, yet the words grew in volume and strength as she stood there, tearing all other thoughts from her mind. Zorro was dead . . . and with him, all her family, all her hope, and all of her remaining life.

The horizon was suddenly outlined in black to her, a black which seemed to seep through the sky, turning individual orbs of it grey before infecting the rest.

Arcadia Flores' right hand never reached her brow. Instead, it followed her body down to the balcony tiles as the night returned to her. She fainted dead away.

*   *   *

The incessant cackling of the wizened old crone in the pancho and rags was finally too much for Sergeant Garcia. "Suela, please!" he begged the ancient woman. "Please, can you not see I have troubles?"

The bent, spindly body stilled. Her lined, leather-like face glanced up at the sweating, rotund soldier who stood alone before the stone of the prison walls. He had sent everyone else away before he studied the damage. The townspeople knew enough to give the sergeant a wide berth in the aftermath of another attack by El Zorro, and his own men knew that the less they knew, the less they would be held responsible.

Only the old woman—the pathetic one everyone referred to with the name that meant the underside of a foot—knew that this was more than just one of Garcia's moods. The aged hag, who most in the town ignored, could see from her years of watching faces that the sergeant had more than anger and fear on his mind. Her long, cracked fingers scratched at the scummy water in the old bucket between her feet as if its surface was the thick fur of a favored pet.

"Of course, of course, *gordo ternero*," she cackled. "You have many troubles . . . more troubles than you have pounds, eh?"

Garcia's hands suddenly snapped up to lay against his girth. Her sardonic description of him, "fat calf," reminded Garcia of more than just his weight. If Captain Monastario heard of this latest humiliation by the night-riding fox, the sergeant might be a lamb to the slaughter indeed.

"Your precious *riqueza amante* may lighten you up some, eh?" Suela continued to chide in a merry sing-song. "When he, your lover of wealth, learns you have let El Zorro make a fool of him and your guards twice in such a short time . . . and all for the beauty of one all want but none possess . . . well, who knows how much flesh he will relieve you of?"

Garcia looked from his belly to the jail, then back to the old woman as she crouched in the shadow between the prison and the barracks. "As the *Capitano* is my judge, old woman, if you did not do the officer's wives the favor of your readings, I swear on the memory of my mother, I would . . ."

"You would what, *gordo ternero?*" she suddenly asked with a broken purring. "Imprison an old woman as you would a beautiful young lady?" Her cracked-tooth smile suddenly took on a sad satire of playfulness. "Do you think El Zorro would come to my rescue to show you the error of your ways as well?" she asked him, her matted hair of straw glinting with oil in the morning sun. "Or would it merely take my plaintive singing to draw the officers' wives to the window of my cell?"

"Now stop this, old Suela," Garcia moaned, holding his head. "Please, I need to think. I do not understand why I let you remain when I find you underfoot."

Garcia turned his worried head away from the prison wall. It looked none the worse for wear following the previous night's fiasco. And, save for a prisoner under a doctor's care for a nasty cut along his forehead, the injuries were not enough to alert the Captain's office . . . not yet. And at least that infernal El Zorro had not decorated every door and wall with his accursed *Z*!

"You know why," the old woman wheezed back. Her cracked, dark fingernails still scratched rhythmically at the dirty water's surface in the old bucket. "Because I can tell you things . . . things that could help you . . . things that you want to know. . . ."

Garcia stilled, the ancient woman's words riffling the many hairs on the back of his bulbous neck. He knew he should not believe in such nonsense, but the officers' wives told many tales of her soothsaying—tales that seemed too accurate to be completely dismissed.

"What do you see there, Suela?" he asked, leaning closer to the old woman. "What do you see in your waters?"

"So, finally, fat one, you are willing to believe in the words of Suela? What would your men say if they heard you asking me to know what images dance on the surface of the water? What would your Capitan say?"

Garcia grimaced, his porcine shoulders heaving once as if to toss her words off his back. Such an insult as "fat one" coming from anyone else might mean punishment and imprisonment. But from her, it was like the wall calling the well mildewed.

"As you can see, wizened crone, my men are not here," he answered with command. "And, as for my Captain, what do *you* think he will say?"

Their wily smiles mirrored each other's for a moment, and then the woman looked down to the top of her bent, coarse bucket, her knotted fingers leaving the water gracefully. But before Garcia could peer into the liquid, the top of the old woman's kneeling head came into his vision. Her disgusting, unwashed hair and ashen, vein-lined skull made him look away.

"Your Captain," she whispered, "will say nothing because, as you had hoped, he will not know. The uninjured prisoners are locked away in the very bowels of your dungeon, while your man of muscles guards them with conspiratorial shame." She looked up at him with a certain sadness. "He had waited all his life to match his strength with that of El Zorro, and when they finally were contested . . ."

"Yes, yes," Garcia interrupted impatiently. "Bajista is crushed. I know. So now he will guard these men's loose tongues with his very reputation, I know. What else do you see, old woman?"

Suela did not return her eyes to the water. Instead, she locked the steel gray of her orbs with the soiled brown of the corpulent lancer's. "I can see your shame, Garcia," she whispered. "I can see the guilt inside you, coiling like a serpent."

Garcia reared back, as if she had suddenly leaped forward to slap him. "W-what? What is that you said, crone?"

"It is a viper inside you, fatted calf," the old woman said, her eyes rising up under her lids, sinking deep into her sockets. "It shall poison you if you do not rid yourself of it."

Garcia bit his suddenly trembling lower lip in a vain attempt to keep it still. "Nonsense!" he blurted. "What do I have to be guilty about? This is . . . this is foolishness!"

"Confess your shame, Garcia," the old woman intoned quietly, beginning to rock back and forth. "Go to the one you trust. Tell him of your guilt. Then you will be free . . . and safe."

"I . . . no! Guilty? Me?" the sergeant muttered, his body shaking as if rocked by small quakes. "Be still, old woman!" He looked away, suddenly seeing pedestrians across the square as if for the first time. "I

. . . I will not listen to this any longer. Be on your way, Suela. Good day . . . good day!"

Then he half-stumbled, half-ran away, back to his office. The people on the other side of the square watched him, wondering why he seemed more agitated than usual. And to a man, woman, and child, they saw only the sergeant. No person who ever spoke of this curious incident to friends or family ever mentioned the presence of a small, bent, emaciated old woman in the shadows . . .

Suela stared back at the unknowing onlookers for a frozen moment. Then their heads followed the movement of the spooked sergeant, the eyes moving across her blind to her visage. Secure that her presence would be but a small, dark hole in their memories, she looked down at the water again.

Her crooked digits stirred the surface once more, parting the scum and algae there in a small circle.

And within the circle, seemingly floating on the surface of the water, was the figure of a beautiful young girl. The dark-haired beauty in the gloriously brocaded gown appeared like a tiny living doll, unconscious in the center of an overgrown lake.

"Sleep, my child," the crone whispered. "Sleep and heal until your mind is strong enough. . . ."

Had Garcia returned and managed to peer where the old woman was looking, all he would have seen was dark, fetid, empty water.

Chapter 11

She is in a what?" Diego asked quietly of his mute manservant again, sitting beside Arcadia as she lay on the beautiful bed.

Bernardo's hands moved through the air, his face serious behind them as he stood at the baseboard of the locked glass doors leading to the unused balcony.

"C-o-m-a," Diego said slowly as he translated Bernardo's movements. "What is this?"

Bernardo tried several more sign language letters before grimacing, erasing them in mid-air and returning to the more universal language of mime. Putting his palms together, he laid his head against them as if resting on a pillow made of his fingers.

"Sleep," Diego correctly assumed.

Then, his face still solemn, Bernardo crossed his fists on his chest and closed his eyes.

"Dead," Diego said somberly. "Sleep of the dead."

Bernardo opened his eyes, then nodded slowly, and sadly.

Diego returned his gaze to Arcadia Flores' tranquil, extraordinarily lovely, face. "I feared she might be in shock after all she had been through," he mused sadly, "but I thought . . . after a night's rest . . ." He looked back to his colleague. "Can she . . . will she awaken?"

Bernardo thought about it for a few moments, then was forced to shrug, moving his palm in a rocking motion. "Perhaps . . . perhaps . . ."

It seemed as if, for a moment, Diego would fall to embrace the comatose woman, but he remained seated beside her, emotions moving across his face like dark clouds. "Night walkers, and now the sleep of the dead," he intoned gravely. "As I endeavor to prove myself, people are standing at the gate of death, and if I do not act they shall surely walk inside . . . and soon."

He felt the hand of his trusted associate upon his shoulder. He covered it with his own. "Thank you, old friend," he said. Then, with a final look at the peaceful face of the oblivious beauty, he rose to his feet in the well-appointed bedroom. "Again," he said. "Tell me everything that transpired from the time you brought Señorita Flores to this room last night. Are you certain she simply cried out in her sleep once?"

Bernardo communicated the facts once more, careful to leave not a detail out. Zorro had been unwilling to secret Arcadia in their caves, so she was brought to his late mother's room . . . a room his father had not entered since his beloved wife's death—unable to imagine awakening to see the beauty of Los Angeles without his wife by his side. Don Alejandro had then moved to another room—one facing the burgeoning city.

To secret Arcadia Flores in this room was yet one more trespass against his honored father, but one Diego was certain the patriarch would forgive him, had he known the truth.

"Do you trust me?" Zorro had asked her.

"With my life," she had replied with fire. "Twice."

He had smiled and said that he would bring her to a house of safety, but for the safety of all, he must keep its location a secret, even from her. She had readily agreed, and allowed herself to be blindfolded. When he had told her that she was able to remove the obstruction from her eyes, she heard the door close behind him and found herself standing in this room.

Bernardo had laid the brocaded nightdress out on the bed, and it was only a matter of moments before Arcadia had discovered it and an adjoining bathroom—the tub filled with warm water and a variety of soaps nearby. Availing herself of all the luxury, it was a wonder she had not dozed off in the bath. Still, many minutes later, she was clean, changed, and comfortable under the covers.

Bernardo had checked on her some time after that, a dim shaft of light from the open door illuminating her sleeping face. Yet, it was at that moment that the mute manservant had heard her cry out three words:

"Zorro is dead."

By the time Diego had been summoned, her exhaustion, trauma, and tragedy had already forced her into this sleep of living death.

They had stood by her bedside since then. Their only knowledge of the sunrise came when they heard the bell for breakfast. At that moment the two men's eyes met. Now, Don Diego stood, angry and confused, facing the painting of his family. He saw the smiles on the faces of his father, mother, and younger self, and suddenly felt a longing he had never known. Fighting this emotion, he turned his head away, attempting to maintain a sardonic smile.

"Happier times, eh?" he said to Bernardo, but then even the forced smile disappeared.

For Bernardo was not looking back at him. Bernardo was not even looking at the sleeping beauty upon the bed. Bernardo was looking upward, in the corner where the walls and ceiling met.

Then Diego heard it as well. It was a quiet, distant lament. But, as he struggled to recognize it—to even hear it clearly—he realized it was somehow much more than a lament. And yet, at the same time, much less than one. It was a song, really. A song that could have been mistaken for a distant bird's cry, or the moaning of wind through tree branches, or even the rumblings of the earth itself.

It was a song, Diego realized with surprise, for the dead and living. A dirge for the living dead!

They both ran from the room, although Bernardo carefully and silently closed the door behind them before his unerring sense of direction brought them downstairs and through the expansive, sunlit, airy kitchen.

"Master Diego!" cried the cook from the central butcher block table. "Will you not join your father for—"

"Soon!" the younger de la Vega interrupted with more mirth than he felt. "Soon, *mi amor*. Please tell my beloved papa not to wait . . ."

The cook watched in minor amazement as the two ran out the back without slowing. Finally she shrugged and turned to her helpers, who were making tortillas. "Those two," she said with a small smile, shaking her head. "What mischief they're always up to. . . ."

Diego got outside in time to see Bernardo scrambling up a rocky incline just below the de la Vega matriarch's room window. It was overlooking the northeast corner of the hacienda, at the most wild and untamed area of the wilderness beyond the protective wall. Despite their long association, Diego couldn't help but marvel at Bernardo's speed and strength as the mute bounded up the hill, then climbed the wall as if it were a ladder.

Within moments, Diego was beside him, and the two vaulted up and over as if the twenty foot obstruction was a mere foot race hurdle. Their fall on the other side belied that impression, however. Each man tested his leg strength and acrobatic dexterity to the utmost as they dropped a full thirty feet to sloping, sandy ground.

Diego slid and rolled, coming up to control his fall like the master athlete he was. Bernardo's fall was more unseemly and clumsy, but the result was the same: both men were on their feet, uninjured, at the bank of a treacherous wood.

Treacherous, because the roots of the forest seemed to grip a series of cliffs like clutching talons. Had the men not regained their balance in time, they would have either pitched over a series of jagged stone stairs—which would have broken bones like twigs and peeled skin like mangoes—or smashed into bent, coarse, twisted trees. Instead, they stood on the top lip of the stones, breathing deeply while listening intently for the strange, hypnotic song.

Bernardo turned his head sharply to the left and the song abruptly ended, disappearing like a popping soap bubble. In its stead came soft, calm words.

"They came years ago," said the old woman known as Suela, kneeling amidst a tree's roots as if part of them, her voice a jagged tear in the air. "They enslaved my people and plundered our city, but that was foretold. What was not predicted was that one man . . . one truly wicked man . . . would know what evil was. It was that man who killed the shaman and stole our true wealth."

She looked up at them, her song at an end, her eyes sharper than Zorro's sword, cutting through them. "They should have killed me as well . . . would have killed me, had I been a man." She smiled then, a smile that chilled the warm Los Angeles morning. "The weak, foolish Aztec betrayers who had led our enemy to the heart of our city thought it would be a bad omen to kill me. They thought I would stain them with my spirit."

She cackled, a delighted crunching sound that made Bernardo cringe. "Modern children," she mused, then looked directly at Diego. "But they were right. I would have stained them—had they lived long enough for me to do so. But the one with the treasure did not want to share. They never do. So all dead . . . all dead except the one they call Suela. . . ."

Finally, then, Bernardo turned to Diego. He lifted his foot and pointed at his sole.

"Yes," croaked the old woman, clapping quietly. "Yes, that it my name and my place to those in this land of angels. But that is not my true name. . . ."

"True name?" Diego echoed, looking from his associate to the old woman. "What is your true name?"

Only then did the woman stand. She stood before the tree, somehow matching its strength and wisdom. "My people knew me as Alma." Alma . . . the Spanish word for soul.

Diego stared at her, looking at the living past—seeing the strength and beauty of this nation before the European settlers came. Even he had to wonder if he was truly worthy to look her in the eye. "Alma," he said. "Why are you here?"

This time she looked only at Bernardo, the man who could not speak. "He called for me," she told him "And so I have come."

"Called for you? How could he have called for you?"

It had taken all of Diego's willpower to remain at breakfast with his father while he knew Bernardo was just upstairs with the strange old woman. Of course he had occasionally seen her in town, but, like everyone else, he had not thought twice about her. Just another old crone, satisfied to spend her life watching those younger pass her by.

And yes, he had heard of her telling fortunes, but what old woman from the village didn't? Hardly a day went by without his hearing of yet another indulgence visited upon the officers' wives by the old crones. Foot massages, tobacco-leaf facial wraps with ancient herbs, new colors of lip and fingernail paints from crushed berries, herbal and wine concoctions guaranteed to help lose weight or keep one's skin looking smoother. . . .

Now the three stood around the bed as Arcadia lay in her sleep of sleeps.

"Have you not heard silence?" the old woman answered the young master of the house with a cracked smile. "Have you not seen nothingness?"

Diego looked once more to Bernardo, who slowly but certainly made the sign language symbol for "trust."

"Yes," Alma said with a sigh. "For, you see, I heard his silent call for assistance to the spirit of the Aztecs. Yet, now, there is only me . . . the one you see but do not see . . . the one to whom none pay any attention . . . the one who goes everywhere to learn everything with all unawares. . . ."

Diego blinked once, feeling a strange resonance somewhere inside him, seemingly in his very soul. And there it was again, the same strange flicker of surprise he had felt when he finally noticed the man he had not seen emerge from the crown of the pyramid in Los Rayos del Sol. It was a surprise that mingled concern, doubt, and perhaps even fear.

Diego closed his eyes and shook his head. That I cannot tolerate, he thought. There is not time for me to be even a sword's breadth afraid. . . .

"No!" the old woman said sharply. He looked up, surprised, to see her glaring directly at him, her steel eyes hard—boring into him from a leathery, creased face. "You must face the fear. You must accept it . . . make it your own."

"But how," he stammered. "I didn't say . . ."

"But I heard you, Diego de la Vega," she replied intently, "as surely as if you had spoken. As surely as the kind, capable Bernardo had called me. For you seek something tangible yet intangible. You seek the room with no walls. You seek the empty mirror."

Diego looked helplessly at Bernardo. But, for his

part, the mute manservant merely nodded. Reeling with warring emotions, Diego looked back at the seemingly fragile old woman.

"You are scarred in mind and body," she warned, "and even your soul is threatened with the jaguar's poison. But only if you allow it."

"Me? But how did I allow it?"

"The hunter did not forcibly enter your mind. You allowed him inside." She lowered her head to look tenderly at Arcadia Flores. "As did she, poor child. . . ."

"How?" Diego asked again. "Can you help her?"

Alma, the soul of her long-dead people, looked back up at the young avenger. "Oh, yes. But first she must rest. And first you must understand. You can only help her, yourself, and your people if you truly understand."

"Understand what?" Diego asked in frustration and helplessness.

Her smile only widened. "Understand that I know what no one else outside this room will ever know . . . that *you* are The Fox, de la Vega," she said. "Cazador, the grandson of the evil one who destroyed my people, is a hunter of foxes. So now you must tell me, El Zorro . . . how will the fox survive?"

"Time has seven children. Each child is an age. The first was the night child: the age of the wildcat. The Earth was in darkness and any human who appeared would be eaten by wild beasts. Horror was visited upon the planet by the nameless child: the age of famine. All the beasts died and the only humans who survived were changed to apes. They lived until the arrival of the Earth child: the age of giants. Mountains rose from the ground, then crashed to the sea. Behemoths were born and died. The planet tore open, and only those with wings survived. They flew through the sky, over the fire child: the age of lava, where the globe was a ball of flame.

"The air child brought calm: the age of clouds. Humans prospered and built, but the air child did not want the humans to be as the gods, so there were whirlwinds that swept the image of humanity away. Then came the water child and the age of judgment. The floods came and all died but two, who lived as dogs but worshipped the gods as the children of time desired them to. Then came the seventh child and the age of elements. He had two hands, which were both closed. . . ."

Alma circled Diego in the cave of El Zorro, telling him the Aztec history of the world, their bodies illuminated by the flickering of a single torch. Diego was seated, his legs crossed, in the center of the rock and dirt floor. He had recovered from the shock of the old woman knowing his secret identity, and was now as certain as Bernardo that she had come not to destroy him, but to help him defeat the evil that was Hidalgo el Cazador.

"Now you must choose one of the hands," she said, walking behind him. "In each there are four elements. In one: Earth, Fire, Air, and Water. In the other: Earthquakes, Famine, War, and Confusion. You must choose one. Choose one now."

Diego did not hesitate. "The right one," he said.

Alma smiled, nodding with satisfaction. "The fox can be fast, but man on horseback can be faster. The fox can be savage, but man with blade or club can be more savage. But the fox will survive by being more wily than the hunter. For that is the fox's power over men. His strength comes with sagacity."

"Sagacity?"

Alma's smile widened. "Yes, my fox, never leave a question unasked, for you seek an answer and a solution. And those never come with silence. Knowledge . . . sagacity . . . comes with answered questions. Now I have a question for you, my fox. What is it you fight for?"

"Freedom." The answer was immediate.

The crone's reaction was as immediate. "No, no, my fox, you were not listening. Not what you fight to achieve for others. What do *you* fight for?"

This time the answer was not so quick in coming. "Survival? Am I fighting for my life?"

Suddenly his eyes snapped open as if bidden. He stared directly into the eyes of the old woman who was kneeling directly before him. All he could see were her eyes, as if her eyes were his entire world.

"It cannot be, my fox," she said sadly. "For life is already yours. You cannot fight for it, or for anyone else. Your fight . . . each and every battle . . . is inside yourself."

He was blinded by the realization. Her world, his world, and all the worlds he had known were swallowed up with the knowledge that he had mistakenly fought for his father, his legacy, his heritage, and his people. To prove to them that he could save them. To prove to himself that he could accomplish this Herculean task. And thereby he had opened himself to bravado, which led to doubt, which led to fear, which led to El Cazador, the hunter, trapping El

Zorro, the fox, inside himself . . . leaving him helpless against the jaguar which raged there.

In that blinding, floating, light-infused moment, he had found the empty mirror.

Chapter 12

Hypnosis," Diego de la Vega read from the leather-covered volume Alma had found in the cave with obvious delight.

"My books, my books," she had exulted, like a woman reunited with treasured stories she had become familiar with as a child. In fact, she was so pleased that the first thing she did upon returning with Diego to his late mother's bedroom was embrace Bernardo and kiss him full on the lips.

After a moment of stunned silence, Diego could not help but burst into laughter, secure in the knowledge that his father was far out of earshot in his salon. Even Bernardo had to smile, delighted that his friend had returned to normal after a trying few days of conflict and failure.

But then Arcadia Flores had stirred in her dream-filled sleep, and all attention returned to her.

"You see?" said the old woman. "She is affected by her inner feelings, reflected from you. Read on, Diego de la Vega, read on."

" 'Hypnosis. A state of imagination induced by suggestion.' " Diego looked up, confused. "That's all?"

" 'That's all?' " Alma echoed, hurriedly pushing down the pillows around Arcadia's head and moving her lustrous hair off her ears. "That's everything! Oh, fools will have you believe it is a living death or bottomless sleep that only the supernatural can achieve, but that is nonsense."

Bernardo and Diego locked eyes for a split second, before the mute one merely shrugged.

"But Alma," Diego pressed, leaning down to try to catch the old woman's gaze. "Señorita Flores is truly asleep, seemingly against her will."

"She sleeps, yes," the old woman agreed, looking up from the young beauty's face. "Lost in her dreams, fantasies, hopes, fears, and desires, but it was at the suggestion of the hunter, Cazador."

"How can that be?"

"It is as child's play," Alma replied dismissively with a wave of her weathered hand. "Post-hypnotic suggestion. Hidalgo el Cazador wants her, for she is truly the most beautiful woman in the town, and beauty is always coveted by the self-loathing. But he would not take her, for then she would be missed by the many whose day is brightened by the sight of her in the plaza." She looked down at the subject of their conversation once more. "So he must convince her to come to him—if not by her own free will, then by other means. . . ."

"The enslavement of her father and brother."

"Yes," Alma said, nodding, "but when that failed

to overcome her survival instinct, he succeeded in pro-
voking a mental confrontation—a stab to the heart of
her brain with a hook . . . a hook that would then
draw her to him at a later time so he could pretend
to be blameless."

Diego straightened, fascinated by the irony of the
situation. "So it seems as if our Sergeant Garcia's
seemingly immoral intervention was a fortuitous one,
eh, Bernardo? Had he not thrown the lovely *señorita*
in his rotting jail, she might already be in the clutches
of our greatest enemy."

"Indeed," intoned the old woman. "But now we
must release her from her mental prison. We must
overcome his suggestion and show her the way out of
her twisted sleep." The old woman stood, looking
across the bed, and its beautiful occupant, to Diego
de la Vega. "Lean beside her ear and call to her, my
fox," she instructed. "Sweetly, gently, but with un-
deniable command. Show her the way home . . ."

Arcadia Flores wandered amidst the wonders of *Los
Rayos del Sol*, marveling at the smoothness of the
path, the richness of the flora, and the beauty of the
architecture. Its flowing lines and deep colors touched
something in her soul, as if unlocking the door to her
eternal memory. She stepped through the rectangular
opening in the Aztec pyramid's base without fear or
doubt, walking between sculptured walls of intricate,
exquisite design.

She saw light up ahead, growing stronger and
brighter with each step, turning the dark granite walls
to a glowing yellow. With a gasp, she saw that the
very path she walked upon was becoming honeyed,
as if liquid gold was flowing beneath her feet. And

when she looked up, a grand sight met her eyes. The inner chamber was huge, filled with many levels and stairways, and adorned with great works of the sculptor's art.

There stood the feathered serpent god Quetzalcoatl, emanating the gentle, peace-loving leadership his people worshipped him for. There were the Sun and Rain gods, whose work brought fertile crops to their lands, sustaining the people. Their images and legends brought serenity to Arcadia's heart and mind as she walked among them. Relaxing as she seemingly had not in eons, she began to hear a song . . . a pure, lilting one that brought her gladness. It was a song which enticed her to follow it to its source . . .

But before she could take another step, the room turned dark, and, as she watched in horror, the Feathered Serpent, the Rain gods, and the Sun gods were replaced in her sight as they had been replaced in Aztec history—with fierce war gods of sacrifice and death. The tribal war god Huitzilopoctli, who rose on a column of flame and whose hunger for corpses was insatiable. Xiutecutli, the fire god and lord of all volcanoes, whose burning eyes witnessed charred bones in his lava flows. And Mictlantecutli, lord of the underworld and ruler of the kingdom of the dead.

The song was drowned out by the roar inside Arcadia's head as these fierce creatures loomed on every side of her. The flames which accompanied them roared to the very top of the pyramid, where the fire broiled across the ceiling. All who toiled within fell around her, writhing in pain. Arcadia stepped back to retreat the way she had come, but she found her path blocked by a sea of bodies. She immediately leapt forward, running toward the yellow light which had drawn her here. Now it cascaded against the far wall, between the erupting gods, forcing her to approach it as her only exit.

She thought she might go deaf with the roar, and mad with the sight of the living gods, but as soon as her foot touched the ball of light between them, the gods disappeared as if they had never existed. Now, their deafening roar was replaced by the clanking and clinking of tools; of axes striking dirt and stone, and of spikes tearing out earth.

She was inside a great hall, a hall torn out from the underground. And standing in the very center of the cave was a man . . . a man dressed in the finery of a living god. "Cazador," Arcadia breathed in dread.

"Yes, my dear," said the man, who wore the feathered headdress, bone-adorned tunic, and the multicolored wrist, head, and leg bands of a demi-god. "In your world I am known by that name. But here . . . here I am known as Tezcatlipoca."

It was the name which meant "Smoking Mirror"— the deity of night and sorcery. "You are not a god," she challenged.

"Ah, my lovely Señorita Flores," he said with a smile, "but I am." He considered her carefully. "Defiant to the end," he decided. "That is but one of your many attributes all which make you worthy of my company."

"Your company?" she spat. "You wish to win me as you would a prize . . . a trophy you can display to prove your worth? You would adorn your arm with me as you would your many meaningless baubles?"

For a moment she thought he would lash out at her, but then he merely sighed. "I shall not force you," he said. "Oh no, not yet. Instead, as would be your wish, I shall leave the decision up to you. Live by my side and share a life of privilege and comfort . . . or stay where you are and join *them!*"

He motioned behind her. She turned to see the emaciated, unwashed, blank-eyed slaves digging weakly at the cave walls. Arcadia stepped back, gasping. She recognized two of them. "Father," she called. "Brother!" And it was at that moment that a single pick tore a hole in the cave wall from which burst a torrent of gold.

The gold smashed into the slaves like a waterfall, breaking them like straw dolls. They flew backwards, washed away by the flood, rolling and twisting and writhing; falling directly at the cowering beauty.

"Join me!" the man-god commanded.

Arcadia Flores spun her head toward him, their eyes locking for a split second filled with unimaginable hate. And then she turned back toward the tidal wave bearing down at her.

She ran toward it, her teeth clenched.

"No!" screamed Cazador as she dove, the tortured faces of her father and brother filling her vision. . . .

"Oro!"

Sergeant Garcia and Don Alejandro both heard it clearly. It was a scream which seemed to cut through the entire house and into their ears. The two men looked at each other, then both ran toward the sound of its origin. Much to the senior de la Vega's chagrin, the rotund soldier was closest to the salon door, refusing to move when the elder man came alongside. Their flight was delayed by several seconds as the two fought to become unwedged in the doorway—the sergeant's girth pinning Alejandro there as if hit with several hundred pounds of doughy flour.

"*Ay caramba*, Sergeant . . ." de la Vega groaned. "Stand aside, would you?"

"I . . . am . . . trying . . . Don Alejandro . . . !" Garcia belched, his arms windmilling uselessly.

But, finally, the smaller, much slimmer man popped through the portal and raced to the stairs—the sergeant huffing and puffing behind him. "By all the gods," Alejandro breathed as he reached the top of the steps. "It came from . . ." He couldn't bring himself to say it. Instead, he ran toward his late wife's room.

Sergeant Garcia nearly crushed the smaller man against the side of the bedroom's open doorway when he couldn't slow his hurtling bulk in time.

"Get off me, you great oaf!" Alejandro exploded, attempting to elbow the gasping, unshaven soldier back. Then both men stared in amazement at the sight inside the well-appointed room.

Diego de la Vega stood in the opening of the glass doors, between the billowing curtains, one arm held away from his body, his hand and wrist covered with a thick glove. Within seconds a handsome falcon landed upon his covered hand, its powerful beak squawking a new cry.

"Diego," his father started, barely able to comprehend the situation. "By all the . . . you . . . ?"

"Why, greetings, my father." He nodded at Garcia. "Sergeant. A beautiful day for falconing, eh?"

"Don Diego!" the Sergeant blurted, unaware of the room's significance. "I never suspected that you would be a lover of the sport of birds."

"Well, Sergeant," Diego replied robustly. "As my father well knows, my manservant Bernardo has been keeping and training birds for some time now. And, given it is such an extraordinary day, we thought it might help me with my recent study of their migratory and feeding habits."

"Bernardo?" Garcia burbled on, just beginning to catch his breath. "But he cannot speak or hear. How can he . . . ?"

"Ah, but he can whistle, Sergeant! You do not need hearing or speech to whistle. And he is quite good, if I do say so myself. Besides, in this capacity, I serve as his ears."

Garcia shook his head in renewed wonder. "Ah, Don Diego, you never fail to amaze me as to the length and breath of your studies. I suppose this is why I came to you this day. . . ."

"Came to me?" Diego repeated. His face took on a puzzled expression. He turned toward the window and waved his free hand. "Bernardo!" He was answered by a clear, sharp whistle. Then he moved his other arm and the falcon flew—off through the open glass doors and out of sight.

Turning casually, Diego pulled off the falconing glove and walked toward the men in the doorway. Otherwise the room was empty.

"Diego," his father began again, his voice tight.

Their eyes met and locked. "Yes father. I was here as I am every day, cleaning the room myself. I . . . I have not let the maids do it . . . since the day of my return." Diego felt no shame, because he spoke the truth.

Alejandro stood straight, his face draining of its anger. "My son . . . this is true?"

Diego nodded, then his voice and expression returned to its lighter air. "And then I saw from the

window Bernardo and his birds, and I thought . . . "
Letting the thought trail off, he turned to the sweating
sergeant, who was just getting his wind back. "Ah,
but Garcia, you were saying you came here this day
to see me?"

"*Sí*, Don Diego, *sí*," the man replied, nodding so
furiously his chins seemed like breaking waves on the
shore of his neck. "I had been advised . . . I mean I
thought it wise to come see you on a most pressing
matter."

"Pressing matter?" Diego echoed. "What pressing
matter?"

Garcia looked sheepishly from the elder to the
younger man. "Well, as you know Don Alejandro . . .
Don Diego . . . our relationship has not always been,
shall we say, amicable . . . but I believe you know that
I try my best, and I am, after all, a man with many
serious responsibilities. . . ."

Diego quelled a laugh, knowing Garcia to be one
of the laziest, least responsible men he had ever met.
But it was this very lack of commitment which made
his presence so vital to the ongoing good works of El
Zorro. So Diego swallowed the irony and listened
carefully.

"And I have always felt that, above all, you are men
of honesty and understanding. . . ."

"Come along, Sergeant," Don Alejandro snapped.
"Get to the point!"

"Yes, yes, Don Alejandro, I am trying to." He
looked beseechingly at Diego. "It's just that," he swallowed hard, "I may have made a mistake imprisoning
the fair Señorita Flores. It's just that what she said to
me about my incompetence could be . . . might
be. . . ."

"Nonsense, Sergeant," Diego said soothingly, interrupting his confession. "As far as I know, you were just doing your job. A man of your importance cannot condone insubordination, whether it comes from one of your guards or from a fair maiden. If we all accepted such behavior, where would we be, eh? After all, giving her time to consider her rash actions was for her own good, was it not?"

"Well, Don Diego, when you put it that way . . . " Garcia started, initially pleased by the support, but remembering the old woman's warning. "But now that Señorita Flores is missing, I cannot help but feel that I might be at least partly to blame . . ."

"What else could you have done, Sergeant?" Diego countered. "Besides, wagging tongues in the plaza say that it is El Zorro himself who whisked her away, and the wicked fox has never been known to harm an innocent Los Angeles citizen . . . especially one so lovely, eh?"

"That is true, Don Diego, but . . ."

"Sergeant Garcia!" The cry startled all three men. The trio turned to see Esteban Díaz standing at the top of the stairs. Diego's eyes narrowed, surveying the lancer's bruised face with a certain silent satisfaction, and noting that not a flicker of recognition for him was alight in the prison guard's eyes. "Capitan Monastario orders you to report to his headquarters immediately!"

"Capitan Monastario?" Garcia's face reddened with chagrin and he immediately started waddling toward the stairs. "Of course, of course, right away, Private, right away." In his haste and embarrassment he neglected to thank or say farewell to the de la Vegas, who were left in the bedroom to hear the two soldiers' laments.

"We looked all over town for you, Sergeant . . . what were you doing here?"

"A vital mission of great importance, Private, I can assure you . . . now, how long has the Captain been waiting?"

Father and son looked at one another, the years from their loved one's death a mere flash of light.

"Father . . . " Diego began.

The old man turned his head. "I thank you for honoring your mother's legacy, Diego," he said quietly. "But I cannot enter this room. Not yet. Maybe some day . . . but not today." And with that he walked away, passing Bernardo in the hall.

The mute looked at his master with concern, studying Diego's anguished eyes as he watched his father move slowly down the stairs. He laid an encouraging hand on Diego's arm, and waited until the younger de la Vega looked down at him before making the sign for "trust," then a small *Z* in the air with his forefinger.

Complete conviction returning to him, Diego nodded, turned, and slowly, silently closed the door to the bedroom behind them. As he pushed the locking bolt into place, Arcadia Flores raced out of the bathroom and into his arms. She embraced him as Alma joined Bernardo by the baseboard of the four-poster bed.

"Señorita Flores," Diego started with surprise, "I . . ."

"There's no need to explain, Don Diego," she said in a relieved rush. "The old woman Suela told me all about it."

"All?" Diego repeated, looking at the old woman, whose eyes glimmered with merriment.

"Yes," Flores continued breathlessly. "How El Zorro left me here and you found me. How you and your servant nursed me through my delirium."

"El Zorro?" Diego interrupted. "So it was he who brought you to us!"

"Yes, yes, of course," the young woman replied. "You were, no doubt, in town, filling your evening with drink and song as always . . ." She suddenly looked up into his face in shock. "Oh, I am so sorry, Don Diego! How dreadfully rude . . . after all you have done for me . . . !"

But instead of seeing reproof in his expression, Arcadia was amazed to see utter delight as Diego returned her embrace with gusto. "No need to apologize, Señorita Flores," he said with honest pleasure, looking back at a beaming Bernardo and the old woman. "No offense taken. Every one in this room . . . everyone in town . . . I suppose everyone in all of California could tell you one thing for certain—that I, for one, am certainly no Zorro!"

Chapter 13

By the time Garcia reached Captain Monastario's office, the word that he had sworn he heard cried out in the de la Vega hacienda was crowded out of his mind by the many excuses he had prepared along the way.

"Please excuse my lateness, Commandante, for I was in the hills, personally tracking down the wily renegade known as El Zorro. . . ."

"Pardon my appearance, Commandante, but I was preparing the strategy with which we will find the escaped prisoners. . . ."

"Commandante, you must forgive my men for the time it took for your order to reach me, for I was conducting a house to house search. . . ."

But all these rationales were lost to the sergeant as soon as he stepped into Captain Monastario's quarters. For there, standing behind the commandante's right shoulder as the superior officer sat at his desk, was Hidalgo el Cazador.

There was no mistaking him. It was not so much his religiouslike robes, trimmed in spotted pelt, which distinguished him, nor was it the deceptively plain boots he wore. It was his superior expression, and, more telling than even that, his gaze. It was a gaze of pure power—one of fervent intensity that relegated everyone else in the room to mere pawns to his king.

"Sergeant," Monastario said curtly, not looking up from the parchment upon which he was writing.

"Commandanto . . . ," Garcia stuttered, his jaw flapping like a flag which had come loose in the wind. "Commandanta . . . I mean, Commandante!" He slapped his right boot to the floor and attempted a brisk salute, but his quivering girth sabotaged his arm, causing him to nearly slap himself in the eye.

Cazador watched Garcia carefully, one eye glittering as if it were made of jagged gemstone. The sergeant could have sworn the man snorted silently in derision, but then Monastario was speaking again.

"So good of you to honor us with your presence, Sergeant."

"Yes, Commandante," Garcia said in a rush. "It was just that I was in the hills, preparing a strategy for a door-to-door search, to find the escaped renegade, I mean, to capture the renegade prisoners . . . !"

"Enough, enough, Sergeant!" Monastario ordered, putting his hands up. "There is no need for such explanations. Your absence has allowed me time to put into writing our agreement."

"Our . . . our agreement, Commandante?" Garcia mumbled, relieved at the opportunity to tear his eyes from Cazador. "But I was not here. . . ."

"Not yours and mine, empty-headed one!" Monastario exclaimed. But then he grew visibly calm. "The agreement between Hidalgo el Cazador and the good offices of the King of Spain."

"W-w-what?" Garcia stuttered. "But I thought you said that the Franciscan padres . . ."

"There is no longer any problem," Monastario interrupted pointedly, continuing quickly to cover anything else Garcia might blurt out. "Señor Cazador has kindly offered his assistance supplying our missions with all the volunteers they might require . . . for only a minor consideration on our part."

"Minor consideration?" Garcia said, trying to keep his knees from buckling, or his lower lip from quaking. "What minor consideration, Commandante?"

Monastario began to turn his head to look up at Cazador, but thought better of it in mid-movement. Instead he grabbed the edge of his desk and spoke through clenched teeth. "Round up a unit of your finest men, Garcia," he ordered. "Arm them well and prepare them to be ready at dawn."

"Dawn?" Garcia yelped. "But, Commandante, to prepare such a contingent in a single night . . ."

"You corpulent lummox!" Monastario exploded, leaping to his feet. "Can you not respond to my direct orders without a whining echo? Is your incompetence and insubordination a bottomless pit? Must you continually embarrass me in front of my honored guests?"

The diatribe was abruptly ended with but a single touch of Hidalgo el Cazador's hand upon the captain's soldier. It was as if an iceberg had descended upon the room.

"Do not concern yourself, Capitan," the man said,

his voice a blade in Garcia's ear. "Under our leadership, he shall learn true obedience soon enough."

Monastario nearly looked over his shoulder and opened his mouth to reply, but, much to Garcia's surprise, his superior officer's lips snapped shut and he sat quickly down.

"Sergeant." The voice was a chill along Garcia's spine. He looked over helplessly at the other standing man. "I have explained to your commandante the need for a unit of fit, well-trained men to complete my settlement. I will need your assistance for but a few short hours, in exchange for which I will lend my support to any project your good Viceroy and King might have in mind for this growing, fertile area. Do you understand?"

For a moment Garcia neglected to reply, so intent was he on the way Cazador's words seem to slip past his ears and bury themselves in his very brain. "Uh, yes, of course, Commandan . . . I mean, Señor Cazador."

Cazador smiled at Garcia's slip of the tongue. "Very good, Sergeant. You may . . ." He took a moment to seemingly remember his place. He looked patiently down at Monastario. "May he go, Captain?"

Monastario seemed to shiver, but it might have been Garcia's imagination. "Of course, of course," the commandante blustered, turning to the soldier. "Get out of my sight, Sergeant!" he bellowed. "And get to work!"

"Yes, sir, my Commandante, right away!" Garcia nearly poked himself in the eye again and ran out of Monastario's office faster than he ever had before. Faster than he ever thought he could. In fact, it wasn't until he was halfway across the plaza that anything

other than putting distance between himself and the
mesmerizing, mind-clouding stare of Hidalgo el Cazador entered his mind.

But as he made his way toward the barracks, Garcia wrestled his thoughts back to his captain. A unit
of the most well-armed, best-fit men? To what purpose? To serve as slave drivers? To police the borders
of *Los Rayos del Sol* to keep out Franciscans? To put
the finishing touches on an Aztec pyramid?

Garcia's trot slowed to a crawl, finally stopping as
he leaned against a hitching post. The sergeant concentrated as he never had before. What had the old
woman told him? That shame was a viper inside him?
That only by confessing to one he trusted would he
be safe from its poison?

But what of Cazador's poison? How had it infected
Captain Monastario? Garcia knew that only wealth
and power motivated his Commandante. He had seen
Monastario's eyes glitter when he had brought him
the stolen jewels from the plaza festival, as promised.
The captain's eyes had glittered like the gems themselves . . . as Cazador's eyes had glimmered in the office. But what jewels had the jaguar man promised
the capitan to secure the assistance of a well-armed,
able-bodied unit of the King's finest?

And then the voice echoing through the de la Vega
house returned to his inner mind. Again, Garcia
heard the word as clearly as he had earlier that day.
The word that had been close in sound to the cry of
the falcon, but not quite. . . .

The word *"oro."* So much like Zorro, but so tell-
ingly different.

Oro . . . the Spanish word for gold.

*   *   *

The whip cracked a millimeter from the old woman's eyes.

"No!" she cried, incredibly plucking the tip from mid-air. Her arm had moved so quickly, even Diego had hardly seen it. "It must crack like the very lightning. It must snap like a bone being blasted in two. The sound must slice into the very soul!"

They stood, once again, in the caves of El Zorro, Bernardo laboring over the sharpening wheel once more, sparks flying about his head.

Diego looked to his silent associate for some support, but saw only the back of his skull haloed in sparks. "*Sí*, Señorita Alma," he said with determination. "*Sí* . . ." Then he prepared to lash out with the whip again.

"Oh, do not flatter me as you would Arcadia Flores with the term '*señorita*,' " Alma replied with an incongruous giggle. "Although I, too, admire the young woman's strength."

"Her strength?" Diego retorted with surprise. "Yes, I suppose to loose Cazador's powerful grip on her mind took a certain strength. . . ."

"No, Diego!" Alma said with such vehemence that even Bernardo felt the slight vibration of the walls. "It is that errant belief that has made you weak . . . that has allowed the hunter to set the cat on your trail!"

Diego stood straight, blinking. "I am sorry, Señora Alma, but I, too, felt his power. . . ."

The old woman shook her head as if to rid it of a buzzing gnat. Then she rose to her full height, her back like the trunk of a mighty redwood. She stalked across the cave floor to stand directly before him, her steel eyes blazing. But when she spoke, the words were a mere whisper . . . a whisper which seemed to sink into Diego's mind like seeds into the hungry earth.

"No, Don Diego de la Vega, you did not feel the hunter's strength. You felt *your own*."

"My own?" the man said with no small wonder.

"Of course!" she chided. "All Cazador did—all Cazador *can* do—is unleash the power of another's mind. It is as I told you before, Diego: suggestion. It is all suggestion, unleashing the power of your own imagination."

"But I saw the jaguars which were not jaguars. . . ."

"Of course you did!" she exclaimed. "Because every one of his suggestions led you directly to that vision." She stared into his confused eyes, finally throwing up her hands and making a *tsk*ing noise. "Come now, Don Diego, did you not tell me that Pedro Morales informed both you and your father that the settlement guards had jaguar-skin cloaks and mantles that were fashioned from jaguar heads? Are not the pouches about the throats of every nightwalker slave fashioned from the pelt of the spotted cat? So once you looked into his eyes with doubt—even concern—about his power, what else do you think he would lead you to see? Bushy-tailed rabbits?"

Realization and growing awareness reentered Diego's expression as the truth finally dawned on him. "Of course . . . !"

"There," Alma said with satisfaction, returning to her place across the cave floor. "So when I said the young woman, Arcadia Flores, was strong, now you know why. Her strength of imagination must be great indeed to create the worlds she experienced. Her strength of will must be great, too, to escape them and return to the real world."

"These worlds, then," Diego wondered, remembering what Arcadia had told them. "Were they as false as the animals I faced?"

Alma shrugged slightly. "It is possible," she admitted. "But it is possible, too, that, in his desire, Hidalgo el Cazador revealed more to her than even he knew. Who knows which caves were created by her imagination and which by his? But it is no matter, Don Diego. She is safe now, back at your villa, away from the hunter's mesmerizing eyes. Now it is between he and you. . . ."

She paused as Bernardo approached Diego's side. The servant silently presented his master with the newly modified blade, which shone in the torch light like liquid silver. Diego tested it for speed, strength and balance, beaming at Bernardo with subsequent satisfaction. "It cuts like lightning," he said.

"And reflects your power," said Alma pointedly. "Try it." She stepped forward, her eyes ablaze.

Diego immediately swung the blade up, its blunt side resting on the bridge of his nose. He stared into the steel, its new silver coating reflecting the image of his own eyes back at him.

"There!" the old woman cried. "You see? Whenever you feel even a sliver of doubt or fear at the night walkers' so-called powers, reflect on your own, de la Vega. For you are truly the night fox, whose cunningness will break their spell with a single snap of your whip, and a single slash of your sword!"

Don Diego grinned back at the inspiring old woman, his conviction renewed. Knowledge was indeed power, and with it, no demagogue could defeat him. But now, as they all knew, came the time for more than knowledge. It was time to put that knowledge to use with preparation.

"Now, Don Diego," Alma urged. "Now!'

The whiplash snaked out across the cave and snapped a centimeter from between her eyes with a crack that rolled across the plain like a thunderbolt.

Arcadia Flores' eyes fluttered, then returned to rest. The distant sound of a thunderbolt entered her consciousness, then, with the whisper of a promise, was gone.

The emotional and physical toll of the last few days was more potent than she could have imagined. After awakening from the post-hypnotic state the old woman had carefully explained to her, she had thought that she would be sufficiently rested, even refreshed. But it was not to be. Alma had continued to say that she might as well have been awake for all the good her dreams had done her. For the post-hypnotic state was not sleep, and in it no victim would ever find rest.

Arcadia had wanted to join Don Diego when he left the hacienda to secure information on her family, but while her mind was willing, her body was still exhausted. Attacked in the plaza, confronted in her home, imprisoned in the dungeon, and assailed again there . . . she was surprised she remained standing as long as she had—especially when the luxurious comfort of this bed was just steps away.

Yes, she knew she should be up, helping the de la Vega family, but she felt certain they were powerful enough to convince Monastario, and even that fool Garcia, of the threat Cazador actually embodied. Far more than she, certainly. She had squandered her one opportunity with empty insults borne of dread and mystification.

So, for the moment, she would rest, secure in the knowledge that no enemy could find her . . . and that, for the first time since Hidalgo el Cazador had come to *El Pueblo de Los Angeles*, she was finally, well and truly safe.

The hand gripped her lower face like a clamp, sinking into her cheeks and sealing her lips as certainly as cement.

Arcadia Flores' eyes snapped open and she looked up, horrified, into the dead eyes of Miguel the Leper.

The wound on his forehead was jagged and glistening, the torn and scratched scab making it look like a third, livid eye.

"So, my little temptress," he hissed. "We meet again."

And then, before she could react, he dragged her up, shifting his iron grip to her jaw, and shoving the cloth he had taken from the adjoining washroom deep into her pried-open mouth.

"Oh no, my lady," he whispered harshly. "I know how beautifully, and how loudly, you can sing!"

Her arms came up to strike or claw, but they were twisted deep in the bedclothes. She screamed in rage and her body surged in the brocaded gown, but she could raise no more alarm than a beached fish.

The cruel man almost laughed, but, instead, swirled a handkerchief behind her head and then knotted it tightly between her full, soft, working red lips. "And now, my enchantress," he taunted, "you cannot call for your beloved Zorro!"

"How?" she choked as he quickly wrestled her out from beneath the bedclothes. "How?" But then, as he brutally threw her to the mattress top on her front, she saw how. Standing by the open glass doors, his expression as blank and dark as the night sky, was a young man. A boy, really, a boy she now remembered seeing skulking in every corner of the plaza over the past few days. She even thought she had glimpsed him through the jail's bars the previous night. . . .

But now she had no more thoughts for the once-crippled boy named Joaquin, as coarse rope cinched her two wrists behind her, the Leper tying her as if she were no more than a prized calf. "There," he growled, spinning her over onto her back. He leered down at her. "You see, my little one? I can be taught. There will be no more fighting from you!"

That's when she kicked him. She would have preferred to permanently bring him down, but the only target available to her in that position was his torso. She would have risked the bottom of her foot to his face if she truly believed she could have connected solidly, but she only had time, and the element of surprise, for one strike. So she smashed her foot, with all her weight behind it, into his stomach.

The Leper made a combined whooping and whooshing sound, like a bellows which had been tromped upon, then he slid across the bed to fall over the side. To her frustration, he brought most of the bedclothes with him, which cushioned his fall and muffled the noise to a mere thump.

Cursing her luck, Arcadia hurled herself forward, off the bed, and charged the door.

The boy was on her like an attacking monkey. His spindly legs encircled her waist and his ankles locked around her middle. One arm was around her throat, while his other hand was deep in her hair, pulling her head back.

She screamed uselessly into the packing knotted

deep in her mouth as he bore her down to the floor—
as if breaking an escaping pony. And then the Leper
was there as well, his face flushed and his expression
angry.

Don Alejandro de la Vega shifted in his sleep uneasily,
but he did not awaken. The servant on duty investi-
gated the small thumping he had heard upstairs to
discover only silence and darkness. Then he remembered the birds Bernardo and Don Diego had been
training inside the very room he thought he had heard
the sounds coming from.

With a shrug he returned downstairs, speculating
that perhaps other birds in the area were returning to
their perches now that the predatory falcon had long
been returned to his cage. He turned toward an open
kitchen window. Perhaps he should venture outside to
see if there was any aviary damage to the hacienda's
outside wall. Once again, however, he shrugged.
There would be plenty of time for that *mañana*. For
now, he would remain at his post.

Had the servant ventured outside, however, he
might have seen the macabre, frightening sight of a
trussed, gagged beauty in a flowing nightgown being
lowered from a second-story balcony by bedclothes
knotted together beneath and around her shoulders.
For the descent, her crossed ankles had been tightly
corded as well.

At ground level, the boy spy known as Joaquin held
her down with skeleton-like hands at her shoulder and
knee while the miscreant known as Miguel leaped
from the balcony.

"And now, my darling one," the latter whispered
warningly. "And now . . ."

He carried her to a waiting cart, where she was shoved amidst a loose bale of hay. The boy crawled in beside her, one hand finding her hair again, the other pressing a dull, rusting, serrated knife loosely against her throat. The Leper sneered at her before covering them with more hay.

"Oh, are you disappointed I would not be joining you myself for your final journey?" He seethed at her wrathful eyes. "I am as well. But even I have learned in this short time not to defy the orders of our new master. His directive was specific; that you were to come to him by your own power . . . in either reality or appearance."

His mouth curled with both triumph and frustration. "So, now, enchantress, with the evidence we have left behind and the fact that there are no witnesses, who is now to say that you did not willingly travel to your final resting place? The place where I now direct this innocent, innocuous cart . . . this cart that no one will suspect hides the rose of *El Pueblo de Los Angeles* . . . the cart with which you will pass, silently and in stillness, beneath their very noses. . . ."

She heard the destination with a dismay which paralyzed her even more than the metal at her neck.

"Los Rayos del Sol."

Chapter 14

Sergeant Garcia was stunned by the sheer number of peasants who appeared around him and his fourteen men as they made their trudging way to *Los Rayos del Sol*. At first they had been merely shadows to the contingent, but as the miles between them and their barracks grew in number, so did the natives— until Garcia compared his voyage to wading through a sea of living water.

But all the tales of this settlement, even magnified in the reluctant, exaggerating mind of the sergeant, did not do the excavation justice. For that was what it truly was—a monumental discovery dug out of the very earth, astonishing for its feats of engineering and artistry. Even the stolid, silent Bajista had to stop, mouth agape at the first sight of the Aztec-style pyramid, encrusted with jaguar carvings, in the waning light of sunset.

It was only after a few seconds that Garcia and his men realized that there were more than just stoop-shouldered slaves—some leaning heavily on walking sticks fashioned from fallen tree limbs—moving down the wide path to the structure's opening. Standing unmoved in the surge of pathetic, impoverished, empty-eyed humanity were broad-shouldered, muscular men with flat, sullen faces, wearing cloaks of jaguar skin and headdresses of jaguar skulls.

And then, there, standing before them—the tidal wave of refugees and workers parting for him as if he were the eye of a storm—was Hidalgo el Cazador.

"Sergeant," he said casually, his voice somehow clearly audible above the sounds of trudging feet. "You have made good time . . . remarkable time for you."

Whether by accident or purpose, Garcia ignored the subtle insult, choosing instead to look at the marching strangers all around him. "Yes, yes, Señor Cazador," he muttered, nodding anxiously as he was patently ignored by all but his affable host. "We have walked for much of the day. I did not want to be exposed in the open when night fell on this place."

To his surprise, Cazador merely nodded in agreement. "You were quite wise, Sergeant," the healer said with a smile. He then whispered conspiratorially, "I have heard that wild beasts roam the dark around here."

It was then Garcia's turn to surprise him. "It is not wild beasts that concern me, señor," he said obliviously, still looking around, "save one fox."

"El Zorro?" Cazador exclaimed with a laugh. "You need not concern yourself about him, Sergeant. Between yourself and myself, I have heard that even

Zorro is frightened of the true beasts which guard this ground." He motioned toward one of the jaguar-shrouded sentinels. "Besides," Cazador continued, "even if El Zorro managed to brave the savage teeth and deadly claws of my guardian beasts, my many chieftains have been given thorough instruction. . . ."

With a subtle signal from his master, one guardian stepped to the side and, with a mighty swing, tore a thick branch completely off a nearby tree . . . as if picking a berry off a bush. The masses marched on, oblivious to the show of strength.

Sergeant Garcia was not oblivious to it, however. He swallowed heavily, his chins quivering. "So, Señor Cazador," he said nervously. "What, then, can the King's soldiers possibly do for you that your own retinue cannot?"

Only then did the healer's eyes become veiled. He raised one elegant hand, and crooked one long finger. "Come this way, Sergeant," he said, "and I will show you. . . ."

Arcadia Flores stood, her legs wide and anchored, against the corner of the room, across from the archway which led to the audience chamber. Her body was covered with the most magnificent of Aztec finery—all lines of color, geometric shapes, faces of beasts, and encrustations of gemstones—forced on her by the vacant-eyed, scrawny women of Cazador's settlement. On her feet were ornate sandals, also decorated with jewels, with straps which laced up her shapely shins.

These same sort of straps were also wrapping her arms, cinching her crossed wrists to the small of her back. These straps, too, encircled her head, beneath her newly washed, flowing mane of hair, holding the stitched, leathery pad in her mouth, clamped between her teeth.

Miguel the Leper stared sullenly at her from where he leaned against the archway, sloshing another goblet of wine in the dim light of the chamber. "Sure," he said irritably, "struggle all you want. Hey, if I had my way, you would even be free to scream . . . but the master felt you might disturb his ceremonies. No one would come to your aid, of course, but you might throw off his concentration . . . and we wouldn't want that, now, would we?"

Arcadia simply continued to stare at him, wide-eyed, like a doe caught in lamplight—seemingly unable to comprehend that she was yet again at his violent mercy.

For his part, Miguel seemed to find absolutely no joy in the situation. In fact, he turned his head away, clumsily sloshing some wine into his mouth, as if trying to forget where he was and what he was doing.

"Would you stop looking at me?" he whined, his words just beginning to slur. "I am not going to touch you . . . such were my orders," he said bitterly. "You cannot escape, cannot cry out, cannot fight—and I am here merely to ensure that you do not disturb the ritual until the master returns for his own pleasure." He emptied the cup of its wine and blindly reached out for the pitcher to refill the goblet.

For her part, Arcadia Flores remained frozen, her body blocking from Miguel's view the jade figure of the jaguar child. She stood directly in front of it, her arms wrenched behind her . . . the minute movements of her wrists invisible in the flickering fire light of the low chamber . . . minute movements which brought the straps of her wrists back and forth against one of the two spiking, carnivorous fangs extruding from its lower jaw . . .

Back and forth, back and forth, back and forth—the sharp edges biting into the leather of the straps, digging, tearing, ripping it away in tiny, tiny chunks . . .

Sergeant Garcia and his men did not think they could be more awed than they had been upon the sight of the Aztec pyramid rising from the earth, but they had been wrong. The audience chamber within was even more magnificent, both for what was complete of its ornamentation and what remained unfinished. On three sides of the enclosure were spectacular examples of the craftsman's art, while on the fourth, upon a bluff of stone and dirt, there lay a huge, round tablet—fully the height and thickness of a man—that had obviously just been unearthed.

Upon its front surface was the carving of an Aztec deity's face—an intricate work of art that put the other sculptures to shame, as if they had been chiseled by unskilled children. And all around it moved a mass of humanity, pouring inside the pyramid as if unloosed by a dam. They crowded inside, fanning out from the huge round obstruction, taking their places as if pre-ordained—each and every face turned toward Garcia and his men with something approaching dulled expectation.

Sergeant Garcia gave a frightened start when Cazador appeared beside him and spoke. "Yes," said the healer, "you are wise to concentrate your attention upon the sacred portal. Magnificent, isn't it? It is the work of the ancestors—a work that we here in this time, sorry and pathetic travelers who came too late to the glory of this world, can only aspire to."

Cazador walked to the work, its stone eyes boring into Garcia, its fierce face and fangs seemingly threatening to chomp him into twisted, bloody bits. The healer's face and body held no fear of it, however, and stood alongside as he would have a trusted parent. "Yes," he continued, "for this is why you were called here, Sergeant. It is your hands and arms and bodies which it cries out for."

"O-ours?" Garcia echoed hollowly, wresting his eyes from it to look to his men for support . . . only to find their faces as drained and dry-mouthed as his. "B-but could not this mass of humanity move the stone as well as we?" he asked, reluctantly looking back to the healer with a weak yet hopeful smile. "Could not your amply muscled chieftains?"

The healer shook his head sadly. "My followers have not the heart," he said, glancing at their sunken forms and empty eyes. "My chieftains have not the soul. It will be only your . . ." Cazador searched the ceiling for the proper term. ". . . Shall we say, innocence . . . that will move our sacred portal."

Garcia looked to the hundreds of wretched peasants around him, then back to the powerful gaze of their leader. It was only then that he suddenly seemed to realize the full import of his position, fighting a fear that was greater than all the petty fears of his life combined. Against his will, he found himself taking a purposeful step back.

"Sergeant!" Cazador's voice was like a dagger in the air. "Do you not know your own destiny? Do you not know why I proclaimed this place *Los Rayos del Sol*?" The healer stepped forward to confront the quaking soldier. "The Rays of the Sun, Sergeant. The Rays of the Sun. Do you not know what they are?" Now his face was no more than three inches from Garcia's own; his eyes locked upon the other's, the orbs beginning to take on the power and intensity of the sun itself. "They are golden, Sergeant. Gold . . ."

Garcia knew it then as surely as the word had been carved on the inside of his eyelids. No wonder Captain Monastario had been so open to Cazador's suggestion. It was the promise of possible untold wealth, not untold field workers, which swayed him. Of course, both men had heard the legends of a great cache of gold in the California hills, but both had long ago decided it was a myth. Not before the Commandante had exhausted Garcia and his men with many fruitless digs throughout the area, however . . .

"The Aztec ancestors knew what we did not, Sergeant," Cazador continued. "They knew of the location of gold . . . more gold than any Spaniard had ever laid eyes upon. And now I, too, have found it, and the only thing that stands between me and the greatest wealth the world has ever known is this sacred stone. . . ." He turned the full intensity of his power onto the Sergeant's fragile countenance. "The stone that you and your men will roll aside for me."

"Roll . . . aside?" Garcia muttered feebly, his eyelids becoming heavy; his eyes themselves becoming clouded.

"Yes, Sergeant," Cazador commanded. "With the strength of a hundred men in each of your arms." He placed a hand on Garcia's shoulder. "You know not of this idol's history. You know nothing of its meaning. You hold no fear of its legend. You are ignorant of its power. So go now, Sergeant. Lead your men. Push aside the stone!"

Garcia stiffened, resolve tightening his face as his eyes grew stony. With a curt wave to his men, he stepped forward, standing directly before the carving without concern. "Take your places, men," he said, his voice stronger than it had ever been before. "You, Bajista, the strongest, beside me. You others, gather on the left side. On my command, push right. Are you ready?"

"*Sí*, Sergeant Garcia," each called out once their hands were placed and their feet rooted. And each was surprised by how much they trusted this jape of a man, this corpulent clown that they often derided in the privacy of their bunks.

The healer looked to each man's face with an expression which could only be called exultant. "Very well then, men," the Cazador-controlled soldier said. "Brace yourselves . . . prepare yourselves . . . !"

"Stop!"

The new voice seemed to fill the room, pressing against each and every person's head. They all turned as one to stare up to the very opposite side of the room, where a wizened figure had separated itself from the mass to stand on the very platform where Cazador had "healed" the Yang Na boy known as Running Antelope.

This person had worn the hooded cloak of a beggar, but now stood erect, throwing the hood back.

"Who are you, old woman?" Cazador bellowed, stepping forward. "Who dare mar the ritual of the revelation?"

"Do you not know me?" the old woman called back, her voice as strong as his. "Do you so soon forget the depraved actions of your ancestors?"

Cazador felt these words like stinging nettles, images of destruction and death crowding his mind's eye. Yet still he did not realize who this meddling old woman was. "You are nothing to me," he cried, waving her away and turning his head to his amassed slaves. "Crush her as you would a bottle fly."

The mob moved as one . . . but only for a single step.

"Stop!" she cried again, and, as one, the mob did.

Cazador was thunderstruck. "You dare?" he gaped. "You dare enter this holy chamber as a servant of *Los Rayos del Sol*, then frustrate the ultimate goal of the settlement?"

The old woman smiled wickedly back at him. "Your words are lost to you now, Hidalgo the Hunter," she cried. "You have lost your concentration. Now my suggestion is as potent as your own. You must face the wickedness of your heritage without your mob of slaves to protect you."

Cazador seemed to shrink inside himself, but only for a moment. "We shall see, old crone," he promised, rising up to his full height. "You there, Bajista, the strong one," he called to one soldier. "Break open that old woman as you would a piñata!"

"No!" she cried as the huge soldier slowly turned toward her. "No!" But still he moved toward her, step, by lumbering step, his meaty hands reaching, his massive fingers beginning to claw . . .

"It seems as if his imagination is not yet sophisticated enough to do your bidding," the mock healer gloated. "Yet he still responds indirectly to the one who orders about his superior. Now what will you do, old woman?"

Staring angrily at the oncoming mountain of a man, the woman reached deeply into her cloak's one wide pocket. "Merely this, slayer of innocents."

She raised a square, black package above her head. "Stop, I command you, stop!" she cried out to him, "Or all you have built here will be destroyed!"

Cazador turned his head abruptly back toward her, his expression suspicious, but uncowed. "What do you have there, crone?" he demanded.

"The making of your undoing," she immediately called back.

Cazador was unimpressed. He knew she could not reach him from that far away, no matter how well she could throw. And, if there was one thing the Cazador family knew, it was explosives. No explosive yet developed was powerful enough to threaten him in a package that size, he decided. Nor would it be powerful enough to effect the stone portal or bring the building down upon them. Certainly she might kill a few dozen followers, but followers were a peso a dozen in this region.

He glanced at Bajista's progress. In a few short moments, he would be within twenty feet of her. Then it would only be a few more seconds before . . .

Hidalgo el Cazador waved the threat away dismissively. "Do your worst, old woman. I shall have no more trouble from you than my relatives no doubt had with your ancestors." And with that, he turned away.

"Very well," the old woman said. With a mighty heave, she hurled the packet at the lumbering, muscle-bound soldier.

Against his will, Cazador cringed. Although his mind knew he would not be hurt, his body instinctively protected itself anyway. And since he was in full view of his followers, the mob of hundreds pressed along the pyramid's walls seemed to cringe as well, seemingly preparing for the worst.

Time seemed to slow down. The only sound within the temple was of the black-wrapped package fluttering in the air. Thousands of eyes watched as it hit Bajista full in the chest.

Chapter 15

The pack bounced off Bajista's massive chest, and fell to the ground with a thud. Nothing happened.

Cazador laughed. "A bluff, old woman? A bluff?" he cried. "What is your name, foolhardy one? I wish to inscribe it on a stone to mark your broken, lifeless body."

"Suela," the old woman said miserably, watching the huge soldier inexorably approach, one huge boot stepping on either side of the black-wrapped package.

"Suela," Cazador repeated. "How fitting. For you are no more than a smear on the bottom of my foot." He turned to his brain-deadened worshippers. "Bring that package to me! The first one to claim it will be rewarded with my approval."

The crowd surged forward, but one rag-wrapped man grabbed the black packet before all the others, then disappeared back into the swelling mob. The movement of the mass seemed to mark the man's progress, the way a deer running through a waving wheat field would mark a trail for its hunters.

"Do not concern yourself that I will be harmed by any trap you have devised, foolish crone," Cazador taunted the old woman, who remained standing, defeated, on the temple platform. "I will have the carrier open the package himself, and show me its contents from a safe distance."

He started to turn away, then thought better of it. "And do not try to run," he advised. "You wouldn't get far with my chieftains protecting this place just outside." The healer seemed to gain great solace from that knowledge. "Yes," he mused. "Not even the most cunning creature of the night could get past all of them. Not even the wily fox."

"I do not need a fox," Suela suddenly cried, "for you have underestimated the power of my ancestors." She looked down into the deadened eyes of the oncoming soldier and spoke directly at him. "Do you not know the face of the god you desecrate?" she pleaded. "Do you not know the power and anger of Xiutecutli, the god of Yellow Fire?"

"Oh, hush woman!" Cazador boomed. "Do you not know when you are defeated?" he said in a tone which mocked her pleading. "What have we to fear from this . . . this face? I know the story as well as you. That before the Aztecs settled in Mexico, they lived far to the north, in a land of fish and waterbirds and gardens. Sound familiar? Is this not such a place? And, yes, of course I know that there they worshipped the sun gods and collected all manner of rock and stone that shone the same color as their deity . . . !"

He spun to face the giant stone, where Garcia and

the remainder of his men remained frozen. "And behind this wall is where they stored those stones. I am certain of it." He took the moment of pleasure to turn back to the old woman. "As certain as I am of the fact that you will die." He called out to the lumbering giant. "Bajista, take her . . . take her now!"

To the healer's confusion, the woman did not struggle when the soldier gripped her in a massive bear hug. Then, to the soldier's consternation, his first crushing pressure seemed not to effect her in the slightest. Nothing was accomplished with the second embrace as well.

"Fool!" Cazador cried. "Do not squeeze. Break her bones! Break her in two!"

Bajista grabbed the old woman by the throat. He grabbed one ankle. He lifted her high above his head.

Miguel the Leper shook the pitcher for the third time. Yet again, no burgundy liquid dripped from the downturned spout. He frowned sloppily, unsatisfied, then looked back to the woman for some sort of solace.

She glowed in his sight like a goddess, the colors of her dress swirling in his vision. Her features were all the more beautiful for his drunkenness. In her wide eyes he saw adoration, not hatred. In her hair he saw the promise of freedom. And in her lips, he saw the sweetness of wine, not a sound-crushing gag.

"Come here," he said, lurching toward her, his fingers clutching. "Come here, you wanton harlot. You know as well as I that this was promised from the very beginning. . . ."

Arcadia Flores, her hands free, brought the jagged jade figure of the jaguar child around with incredible speed, driving its sculpted fangs and claws directly into Miguel the Leper's face.

Bajista blinked.

The sharp, loud, snapping sound followed the movement of his eyelids as thunder follows lightning. Then, before Bajista's stunned gaze, he watched as his eyelashes fluttered to the temple floor.

The big man cried out like a child, suddenly feeling the pain above his sight. He dropped the old woman, his meaty hands going to his face. Suela landed nimbly on her feet, then expertly rolled across the temple platform to stand behind it.

Cazador saw it first as a swirling shadow. A shadow which detached itself from the mob like flowing oil, a glint of steel emerging from the center of its gnarled, bulbous, wooden walking stick. Then it took shape, turning from the crying soldier to face him, cape swirling, a shining sword in his left hand, a coiling whip in his right, his eyes ablaze from behind a mask of black silk.

"Zorro!" Hidalgo el Cazador cried.

The renegade horseman made a small, stately bow. "At your service, Don Hidalgo," he said calmly. "Thank you so very much for giving me time to change. It is good to finally meet you face to face. Especially after I have heard so much about you. . . ."

"But how?" the healer blurted. "How did you get past . . . ?"

"Ah, but the fox has many disguises," Zorro said. "And how best to hide amongst pilgrims but as yet another pilgrim? But the time for talk is done, my dear fellow. Now the fox has come for the hunter!"

And then, from beneath his cape, emerged his grenades.

Arcadia wrenched the gag from her mouth and fled toward the archway, only to have her way blocked by the boy Joaquin. He stood there, silent; his back bent, his face tense, his arms wide, his hands ready to prevent her escape—the dull, rusty, serrated blade gripped in his fingers.

"Oh no, my child," Arcadia moaned with honest sympathy. "Please, you have chosen the wrong leader. . . ."

"He," the boy croaked uncertainly, "he healed me!"

"So you could stalk and abduct and hold me prisoner?" she asked him forcefully. "Are those the actions of a savior, or a sinner?" Arcadia saw indecision enter his eyes, but that didn't affect the passionate truth of her following words. "Please . . . you must know what he has planned for me. Can you allow that? Can you live with that?"

The boy bit his lip, but he could not forget the joy in his mother's eyes and the words of celebration she showered on him about the healer's "miracle." Tortured, unsure, blinded by fear, the boy charged.

Arcadia gripped his knife arm with the strength and certainty she brought to tilling her family's field. With a twist of her body, she hurled the boy over her back and shoulder, propelling him into the wall behind her. Joaquin slammed into the barrier, smashing more delicate works of the jade sculptor's art, and landed atop Miguel's still, raggedly breathing form.

With the speed and strength of youth, the boy bounded to his feet, crunching the remains of the jaguar-child beneath his soles. With the speed and strength of a veteran farmer, Arcadia punched him full in the face with her open hand.

Joaquin's head snapped back, scarlet liquid from his nose spinning in the air. Arcadia stepped back, preparing to strike him again. But when his face lowered, something in his eyes was different. She froze in place, watching him carefully.

Running Antelope stared at his hands, then slowly turned his face to her, his mouth and eyes wide. He tried to speak, but couldn't. Suddenly he started to cry—freed from his spell of deception and treachery—big round tears silently flowing from his eyes like a cleansing rain. A moment later he fell into her arms, sobbing.

She stood there, cradling him, making soft, soothing sounds for them both.

The audience chamber was in deafening chaos; peasants racing in every direction in terror, the chieftains wading amongst them. They angrily swung their clubs and struggled to reach the man in black who spun in the temple's center, his whip snapping into faces, the side and back of his sword slapping against skulls.

His explosives still crackled and whistled and burst all around them—colorful and harmless as fireworks, but more effective than serum. With each crackle of magnesium, snap of copper, whistle of potassium, snap of the whip, and strike of steel, El Zorro was releasing the haunted minions from the spell of suggestion as surely as if he was pouring antidotes down their throats.

"Push!" Cazador shrieked at the soldiers above the pandemonium. "Push as if your mothers' lives de-

pended upon it!" He looked over his shoulder in panic
to see just how close the fox was getting. Judging that
the mob and his guards would keep them apart just
long enough for him to force these still mesmerized
louts to unearth the treasure, his lips curled in angry sneer. Once revealed, who knew what weapons
or escape routes waited for him within?

Zorro spun in a dance of life and death, his sword
and whip unerringly separating the innocent peasants
from the guilty chieftains. For the former, his lash
would snap a hair's breadth before their eyes and the
sides of his blade would slap their cheeks. For the
latter, the whip would slice and the blade would cut.

The channel Alma had opened between his body
and mind invigorated him, giving him a strength and
speed he had never called on before. His lips moved
back off his teeth in an exhilarated, determined smile,
until he spun around to face the slave master of the
Los Angeles hills.

He was just in time to see the soldiers accomplish-
ing their corrupt goal. They had managed to move
the obstruction. A sliver of light emerged from the
crack they created between the stone and the cavern
within. Blinding, bright yellow light flooded the temple like a beam of sun entombed on Earth. Even the
chieftains had to shield their eyes and move back. But
Zorro merely nodded his head, bringing the rim of
his black hat down to create a visor that protected his
vision.

"More!" Cazador screeched. 'Just a few inches
more!"

"No!" Alma cried, leaping upon the bluff where the
soldiers strained.

But it was too late. With one final, all-encompassing

push, the rock rolled aside. The sun-bright light from
inside diffused to fill the pyramid, but not threaten
blindness. Even so, almost all but Zorro had to blink,
reeling from the explosions of gray nothingness which
filled their vision.

The scene which met his gaze when he raised his
head was almost too much to bear. For his trusted
Alma was, for at least an eternal moment, stunned by
the wealth she witnessed. Perhaps she had expected
piles of gold. Perhaps she had thought it would be
chests of golden coins. But no one had imagined that
it would be a room of solid gold, with every wall, inch
of floor, and even stalactite and stalagmite shining
with the most pure of golden liquid light.

And it was in that eternal moment that Zorro saw
Cazador pull the jewel-encrusted knife from his cloak.

"Alma!" he shouted in warning, leaping forward.
He had time; he knew it. This tragedy would not happen as long as the speed and strength she bequeathed
him remained.

But then he was stopped in mid-air—meaty hands
blindly gripping him, holding him, pulling him back,
pinning his arms to his side, crushing him. . . .

"Bajista!" Zorro howled in fury as the stunned,
blinded, yet still powerful oaf attempted to destroy the
fox in one mighty, spasmodic grip.

Zorro's head snapped back, breaking Bajista's nose.
His feet flew back, his boot heels breaking bones in
both Bajista's knees. His sword swirled in his pinned
grip, the the blade slicing upwards to snap at both the
giant's gripping hands.

Bajista released him, his knuckles and fingers ruined. Zorro jumped forward as Alma fell, her rags
stained with dark liquid.

Behind him, Bajista also fell to his ruined knees, the crackle of those shattered bones echoing against the wall, only to be drowned out by the man's screams of pain before his loss of consciousness.

"Alma," Zorro said with sorrow as he crouched over her fallen, tiny body. He tenderly held her weathered, pain-wracked head up with one gloved hand.

Her withered lids fluttered and then the steel of her eyes shone again . . . a shine that was dimming even as Zorro watched. "Ah," she whispered, "my fox. My dear, dear fox. I am so sorry. I . . . have you done as I taught you?"

His eyes were hot as he answered. "Yes, my Alma . . . my soul. Your people will be free."

"Good," she said, almost too softly for him to hear. "That's good. For, in a moment of blindness, I am assured of joining them." Then she managed a final smile as the finger of her right hand fluttered. "El Zorro?" she breathed warningly, "Chieftains . . ."

He looked up to see the remaining members of Cazador's guards pushing through the stunned, wandering masses toward the golden cavern opening.

With an angry movement of his arm, Zorro brought out another one of Bernardo's specially-made grenades. He lit it with a deft twist of his fingers, and hurled it—practically in the same motion. Not at the chieftains, but at the still comatose Sergeant Garcia and his men.

Zorro crouched in the sparks and light shafts as the fireworks explosion momentarily stilled the chieftains' charge and woke the Spanish lancers in no uncertain terms. The fox only raised his head when the worst of the detonations were over.

"What? Where are we? How did this happen?" the sergeant sputtered, looking in every direction as if awoken from a nap by a bucket of water.

"Garcia!" Zorro commanded. "Stop those guards from harming this old woman further!" It was the steel in the voice the sergeant immediately responded to, as Zorro knew he would.

"*Sí*, señor," Garcia said automatically, not even re-alizing what he was saying or who he was saying it to. "Men!" the sergeant called, still somewhat deliri-ous from his experience. He surveyed the scene and decided not to use the rifles in such a confined space. "Swords unsheathed," he ordered. "Attack position! Charge!"

The men leaped, screaming, off the bluff to engage the stunned chieftains amid the confused mob. All of Garcia's frustrations, doubts, and shames of the past days exploded through his body and arms as he swung his rarely-used sword like a man possessed. The ser-geant fought as he never had before . . . and perhaps as he never would again, the hypnosis returning to him the strength of his long-forgotten youth.

As Garcia deliriously fought in the diminishing ech-oes of his trance, Zorro gently laid to rest the head of the last Aztec shaman. Then he stood, his back to the warring mob, his eyes filled with the hunter's gleam-ing lair. Sword in one hand, whip in the other, El Zorro stepped into the rays of the sun.

Chapter 16

As he had expected, the jewel-encrusted blade had come at his face like an angry, deadly wasp as soon as he emerged in the glowing cave of gold. As he had not anticipated, his responding sword had been deflected by the low ceiling. Zorro had to pull his head abruptly back so that the wasp's sting would not draw blood.

His other arm shot forward, his whip sizzling toward the knife's source like a striking adder, but it, too, was frustrated in its quest by obstructive stalactites. It was only Zorro's well-trained reflexes and instincts which kept him from death in the very first moments.

He nearly stepped back into the temple, but the sound of Cazador's diminishing laughter drew him forward, his eyes struggling to adjust to the glowing cavern interior. It was gold, all gold, shining like liquid wherever his eyes moved. It took distinct seconds for him to even make out the curved, narrowing confines of the cave . . . seconds he could not afford to squander.

"So, El Zorro," Cazador taunted from behind some curve within. "You think you have cornered me in my lair? Ah, but when has the fox ever cornered the hunter?" And then the knife bit at him again.

Zorro pulled his body back, bringing his arms forward, to avoid the blade which snapped at his torso. Even so, it just managed to touch his shirt, making a tiny hole that barely avoided ripping skin. His sword and whip were futile in the defense, slapping the golden cave walls uselessly.

"Come, come," Cazador chided, his voice echoing slightly, drawing Zorro further in. "You will never capture me with cowardice. Do you really think you could simply wait for me to come out? But what if I do not? No, my dear Zorro, you will never know how far this golden tunnel stretches until you explore it for yourself. . . ."

Zorro silently cursed the false healer for his caustic truth. He could not retreat now, no matter how difficult the circumstances—not when Cazador might simply disappear, only to resurface elsewhere in the wide, beautiful country, his evil now supported with untold, unknown wealth.

So Zorro stepped forward, and, with that step, turned a short curve in the cave, closing off from even his peripheral vision the last sliver's sight of the pyramid's temple. Now he was totally immersed in gold, his eyes struggling to make out from its shining glare any glimpse of Cazador's magnificent Aztec robe. . . .

There! He saw it, its colors shifting against the left

wall. Like a striking bolt of lightning, his sword pinioned it, biting deep. But it only took a split second for Zorro to realize that this was a false, empty target . . . that his sword buried itself in cloth only.

And then his right arm was moving reflexively, the lashing whip just barely able to divert Cazador's knife point. Even so, it bit into his upper arm, tearing silk, finally drawing blood.

Zorro clenched his teeth and moved back, angry at himself for being fooled by such an obvious stratagem. Cazador responded by laughing again, while moving even further back into the cave's recesses.

"Come along, foolish little fox," he called softly. "By all rights, this should be your warren. Instead, it will be your crypt."

Zorro pushed his sword forward, twirling it in the enclosed space, trying to force Cazador to at least keep his distance. But suddenly, the side of the blade was hit by a golden, ball-shaped rock, knocking the sword into the wall, twisting Zorro's wrist and stinging his palm.

"Ha!" Cazador cried. "What good are your weapons now, fox? In this enclosed space they are only a detriment!"

Zorro could not avoid acknowledging the healer's words. With renewed determination, he laid his sword and whip down on the blinding, golden ground, and moved quickly forward, hoping to match Cazador hand to hand.

But the villain did not wait. Suddenly a pale shape roared forward, sweeping into Zorro's hazy view. And in the middle of the encroaching shape was a sharp, bright, stained steel point which glinted red and green and blue at its base—the jewel-encrusted knife which ended the shaman's life seeking Zorro's very throat.

With the sweep of one arm, Zorro blocked the knife thrust, pushing it harmlessly to the left of his head. But then there was a sharp, pinching pain at his left upper forearm, as if Cazador had gripped his muscle tightly between his thumb and forefinger.

To Zorro's amazement, he felt his left arm go numb.

He wrenched his body back, stunned at the attack. His right arm gripped his left shoulder, quickly massaging, but it was too late. His left arm was dead to him. He stared up into the golden haze, his mouth agape.

"Oh yes," said a pale, wavering shape not five yards before him. "Yes, yes, yes, my dear Zorro. What you now feel, and what you are soon to feel again and again, and again is an ancient Asian art . . . one which I learned at the feet of great Chinese healers. But while they utilized the art exclusively for healing, I use it to seal your demise!"

And then the knife filled Zorro's vision again while clutching, deadly fingers sought his neck. Zorro fell back, his right arm swinging and his legs kicking. He felt the knife rip his right boot, and then fingers clenched just below his knee.

His right leg fell to the cavern floor, feeling like a useless sack of peppers. Zorro stared up, propped on his right elbow, to watch grimly as Cazador took shape before him, his right hand holding Zorro's own sword.

"See how it shines in the golden light of my riches," the false healer jeered. "Did you ever think, crippled fox, that your own trusted weapon would be the cause of your undoing?"

But Cazador's smile disappeared when Zorro merely answered in a tone of voice which gave no hint to his whirring thoughts. "Of course not, hunter," he said casually but clearly. "And nor will anyone else. When they find me, they will assume I fell upon my own blade in the heat of battle. Never for one moment will anyone accept that one such as you defeated me. After all, what do the unwashed masses know of ancient Asian arts?"

"What?" Cazador exclaimed, the point of the sword targeting Zorro's heart. "Do you think you can deter me with mere words?"

"Of course not," Zorro began, and then his left leg moved, trapping the sword between the side of his left boot and the golden wall. Then, with a supreme effort, Zorro hurled his body up in such a way that it propelled his deadened right leg into Cazador's face. Even then, he did not slow. His strong right arm shot out, speeding for Cazador's solar plexus.

But then clawing fingers shot out from the golden haze, clamping painfully onto Zorro's right wrist, then twisting. Zorro grimaced, his teeth clenched, as he felt his blood flow alter and his bones misalign. He fell back, and Cazador fell with him, his light gray tunic and trousers finally taking focus.

Zorro stared up at Hidalgo el Cazador's face, now no further than twelve inches from his. The false healer's expression was one of derisive triumph. With his left hand, he gripped Zorro's throat. With his right, he held up the jewel-encrusted blade.

"So, foolish fox, you will get your wish after all," he scoffed. "Your last wish, eh? Now there will be no doubt as to who brought down the great El Zorro!"

Zorro stared up at him.

"What are you looking at, condemned one? The face of your executioner?"

Zorro stared.

"The face of your true master?" Cazador continued, a mist of confusion touching the very edge of his mind. "The face of your very god?"

Why was he blathering so? Just kill the interloper, take all the gold you and your remaining men can carry, and escape. . . .

Zorro stared directly into Cazador's eyes.

"Why do you . . . ?" Cazador started. "What . . . ?"

Then the eyes of a jaguar opened between them on the cavern wall.

"No!" Cazador gasped, gripping Zorro's throat tighter. "It cannot be! Only I—only I have the power to—!"

But the jaguar's angry face was already taking shape in both their sights, looking hungrily from one to the other.

"No!" Cazador repeated, staring back at the fallen fox. "You do not have the power. Only I have the true power of mind control. I, not you! Me! Me!"

He stared back intently at Zorro's determined face, but his gaze wavered when the jaguar stepped out from the golden wall, its spotted tail lashing back and forth in anger—a low growl emanating from its powerful throat. . . .

"It will be you that will feel its slavering fangs," Cazador hissed between clenched teeth. "Not I. It will be you who dies. This I promise."

The false healer tried to crush Zorro's throat. He tried to plunge the jewel-encrusted blade into Zorro's heart, but it was as if his arms were frozen in time.

Zorro said nothing. He continued to stare.

"No," Cazador said, his voice now a hoarse, concentrated whisper. "Not now . . . not now that I have achieved my ultimate desire!"

And then Zorro's words stabbed into his mind as if they were the jeweled blade. "Your words are like my arms, Don Hidalgo," he said softly. "Useless. They will not support you. They are but upheld hands to fend off a flood. Your cause was unjust, so you will be consumed. This is your rightful punishment. You know it as well as I. . . ."

"No!" Cazador screamed, his head back, the sound echoing off the golden cavern walls.

The jaguar pounced, its fangs finding Cazador's throat, its claws tearing at his torso.

Zorro dragged himself up the cavern wall, using what power was left in his arms and his still-strong left leg. He stared down at Cazador, who rolled about the floor, screaming, clawing at his own throat and beating at his own body.

Even as he watched, Zorro felt strength returning to his insensate limbs, as if his blood flow was crashing through internal barriers and his skeleton was automatically correcting its bone pattern. He quickly retrieved his sword, finding it against the rear wall of the cavern. So, he thought, feeling the smooth sheen of the enclosing gold, there is no escape route after all . . . there was but only one entrance.

He ran back, leaping over the still writhing, shrieking healer. Zorro gathered up his whip and raced with all his strength toward the entrance, reaching back beneath his cape as he went.

He finally turned the last corner, welcoming the sight of the pyramid temple, its dark hues filling his vision like soothing medicine for his tortured eyes. But then he noticed Sergeant Garcia and his men, standing before the entrance like a firing squad, their rifles at the ready. Behind them lay the fallen bodies of the warring chieftains, and beyond that, in the pyramid entrance, the curious faces of the slaves.

The last thing he saw before returning his attention to the lancers was the lovely form of Arcadia Flores, standing in the entrance to the audience chamber, her arm over the shoulder of a weeping young man.

"Surrender, El Zorro!" Garcia cried, his sword raised. "We have vanquished our foes, so there will be nothing and no one to prevent us from finally capturing you. There is no escape. Give yourself up at once!"

"Of course, my dear Sergeant," Zorro called back, his hand swirling inside his cape. "You have my every assurance that I will take you up on your kind offer. But first I must rid myself of but a single inconvenience." He held up a final grenade, its fuse already enflamed. "I'm sure you understand."

Garcia's eyes widened, his jaw working, but his next word was not "fire." Instead, as Zorro surmised, they were "Watch out!"

The soldiers hurled themselves to the ground as Zorro threw the bomb back into the cave and dove out the opening.

Cazador family aside, Hidalgo knew less about explosives than he supposed. With the deeper knowledge of Bernardo, there was more explosive power in Zorro's grenade than the false healer could comprehend. This was no packet of fireworks.

It detonated mid-cavern, smashing the walls and crumbling the ceiling. A huge, billowing cloud of dirt and gold dust belched from the opening, spinning aside the round, rock obstruction which served as its portal. The sealing stone wavered on its edge, then came crashing down on the side of the bluff. It broke in five pieces, scattering amongst the dirt.

Zorro fell to the ground below the bluff, somersaulting, then came up running as rocks and stalagmites shot out from the explosive concussion like cannon fodder and viciously hurled spears. The slaves in the pyramid entrance gasped and fell back as the soldiers held their heads in the mud. Zorro rolled to the side and came up crouching, one arm over Arcadia's back as she knelt, and the other arm holding up his cape over all three of them.

"Come," she heard him whisper.

When Sergeant Garcia looked up, he was covered in an inch of gold and brown silt. His men were already on their feet, running around errantly, their rifles searching for some target. Garcia spit muck from his lips and immediately shifted, looking instinctively behind him. He saw Zorro running toward the pyramid entrance, holding the hand of Arcadia Flores who ran just behind him. At the corner of his eye was a young boy who also ran, but toward the opposite side of the entrance.

"There!" Garcia bellowed. "There! There goes the fox!"

But it was already too late. Zorro plunged into the mass of humanity just outside the entrance and was swallowed up in the crowd, as was the beautiful young girl a moment later.

The soldiers stared back at their sergeant, dumbfounded. "Well, don't just stand there, you fools!"

Garcia cried. "After him! After him! Look for his ebony horse! On the life of my family, they shall be astride it. Go! Go!"

The men went stumbling on their way, the hypnotic spell that galvanized them completely gone, the strength of their mesmerized state as ravaged as the golden cave. Garcia started to push himself up, but found himself staring at a broken stalactite that rested near his right hand. Garcia gripped it in wonder, realizing that it was not solid gold. No, instead, it was made entirely of cave stone, with only its very exterior covered in golden ooze. Even as he gripped it, gold flecks were dropping off it like dead skin . . . leaving only a bone of stone behind.

Garcia clumsily heft his bulk from the ground, somehow finding his feet. He blinked the dust from his eyes, and stared at the collapsed cavern. He shook his head in pity, wondering how he would tell the Commandante that he had uncovered a cave of gold . . . only to let it slip through his fingers.

He looked down at the ground. Already the winds were blowing what little gold dust that remained into nothingness. As he watched it disappear, his explanation of the cave's existence also began to dissipate. Well, he thought, perhaps no explanation was necessary. Whatever promises Cazador had made Monastario could have been as smoke—a clouded mirror with which to reflect the captain's innate greed.

"But, no, my Capitan. It was lies, all lies. I saw no cavern of gold. And neither did my men. Did you, men?"

Yes, Garcia thought with satisfaction. It would be many years yet before anyone found gold in California!

Garcia attempted a weak smile, certain that this explanation would hold up as long as the cave was well and truly sealed. He examined the entrance carefully. Then his eyes widened and his jaw dropped open. It could not be! But yes, it was.

When the explosive collapsed the cavern, it jarred loose three great stones, which served to permanently shut the entrance. These vaguely triangular stones had fallen against one another, each locking into place with their pointed ends opposite the other's. So when they came to rest, they created a clear, obvious seam. That seam ran straight from the left to the right along the top, slashed down from the top right to the bottom left, and then straight back from the left to the right at its base.

Sergeant Garcia stared in astonishment at Hidalgo el Cazador's tomb . . . sealed with an unbreakable *Z*.

Chapter 17

Don Diego!" Arcadia Flores cried with pleasure, waving from the doorway of her family's new hacienda. If anything, she was more beautiful than she had been when de la Vega had first set eyes on her all those months ago. Her experiences had brought a strength of wisdom to her features, and her ordeal had made her subsequent happiness all the more treasured.

This was not the same señorita who had mercilessly chastised Sergeant Garcia, to her own ultimate detriment. This young woman was just as passionate and compassionate, but this one knew that honey would attract more consideration than hot chili.

Her brother and father, too, looked far better than Diego had ever seen them. The intervening months cultivating this fertile land had returned the strength to their withered limbs—as had the exceptional meals of their new cook. That self-same cook now appeared in the doorway behind Arcadia as she ran to the carriage upon which Diego sat beside Bernardo. The older woman was cleaning her hands with her apron, smiling with satisfaction at her young mistress' energy.

She then turned to smile with equal pleasure at the sight of her son working cheerfully in the fields alongside Arcadia's considerate father and helpful brother. Running Antelope was now unrecognizable from the twisted cripple or feral spy he had been under Cazador's cruel tutelage. He was a handsome, strong, happy young man, who would no doubt be a formidable gentleman as the years went on.

"Ah, Señorita Flores," Diego said smoothly, his smile mirroring her own in pleasure. The sight of her and her family reminded him of all the happy reunions he had witnessed in the wake of the Aztec settlement's destruction—not the least of which was when Paulo had returned to the home of a grateful and relieved Don Pedro Morales. "The soil of your new abode is proving bountiful, I trust?"

"Oh, Don Diego," she cried, laying her hands on his arm. "My family cannot thank you enough for allowing us to cultivate this land."

Diego waved the gratitude away with his free hand, enjoying the feeling of her fingers on his now fully recovered limb. "Not at all, señorita. It is your family who does me the service. I couldn't think of a more conscientious group of farmers to make this land come fully alive. Besides," he continued in a quieter, more intimate tone, "it is the least our small *pueblo* could do for you and your family after all you have suffered and all you have done for us."

It was Arcadia's turn to be humble. "Oh no, Don

Diego, my contribution, and that of my family . . ." She looked from the cook to her son. ". . . my entire new family . . . was as of nothing. It was Zorro!"

Diego quickly interrupted. "You need not be so modest, senorita. *My* entire family will always be in your debt." He said this with particular gusto, recalling their fascinating times in his late mother's room . . . and the fact that when he had left the de la Vega mansion for this journey, the door and windows of her tranquil chamber were again open—his father standing contentedly in the air and light of the place, his face finally reflecting the happy memories he had experienced there.

This feast of gratitude was thankfully truncated by Bernardo, who touched Diego's sleeve, then made the sign for "urgency." Diego smiled and nodded. "But of course, my friend. You are right. It is time." He turned back to the lovely young woman. "Are you sure you wish to accompany us, señorita? I do not wish to remind you of any painful memories."

Her reply was friendly but firm. "I insist, Don Diego. Although I know her for a very short time, I will never forget her kindness to me, and the wealth of wisdom in her eyes."

Diego immediately hopped out of the carriage and chivalrously offered his arm to help the young beauty inside. "Then if you would do me the honor, señorita. . . ."

They drove up to the site where the Aztec pyramid once rose amongst the trees. All that now remained was a mound of dirt, stone, and adobe brick—all somewhat viciously harvested by soldiers under the angry direction of Captain Monastario himself. It was, as he said, a job of complex inspection he could not trust to the likes of the bumbling, hapless Sergeant Garcia.

But whether under the command of the sergeant or the captain, the examination produced not a thimble full of gold nor any other precious medal. Hidalgo el Cazador's venal dream was as the dirt beneath their wheels—his lust for power and wealth swallowed up by the land he so abused. The three got out of the carriage near the very apex of the crumbling mound, standing in the sunlight of midday, surrounded by the natural beauty of the lush and fertile land.

While Diego and Bernardo looked down, their expressions reflective, Arcadia looked out toward the horizon, the wind blowing her hair and dress. Finally Diego became aware of her wistfulness, and touched her shoulder. "The fox is a creature of the night," he told her softly. "And, sadly, he must ride alone."

Arcadia Flores blinked, as if something in the wind had touched her eyes, then turned to Diego with a wistful yet secret smile. "Of course, Don Diego. I know that in my mind." She looked away a final time. "But in my heart . . . ?"

"Someday, señorita," Diego told her with a sardonic smile, "your heart and mind, as all our hearts and minds, will be free of the yokes that imprison and oppress them. Maybe at that time, the fox will emerge from the darkness into the light. But until that day . . ."

Arcadia looked down sheepishly, then back to Diego with renewed serenity. "I know, señor, I know. Until that day, I must be strong and loving for myself—not for him."

Bernardo nodded . . . then opened his hand and presented Arcadia with a flower.

"Come," said Diego. "We must return you to the warmth of your loving family as soon as possible."

They walked to the very top of the mound, unspoiled California landscape stretching out all around them. Diego took a deep breath. "It is said that a long time ago the seven tribes of the Aztecs lived in Aztlan," he said, "the white land, until one day a shaman walking amongst the trees heard a bird calling *'Tihui . . . tihui . . . tihui.'* He stopped to listen and realized the bird was calling out in the Aztec tongue, 'Let us go, let us go, let us go . . .'

" 'What can it mean?' he asked his chief. 'The bird is wise,' the chieftain said. 'We have enemies in this place and it is time to find another land. This bird speaks for the gods and the time has come.' " Diego reached into his pocket and pulled out the jewel-encrusted knife with the stained blade. Kneeling, he plunged it into the dirt until it was all but gone from sight. "Travel well, my soul," he whispered. "I shall see you again in the eyes of every resourceful serpent and in every soaring bird."

Then the three returned to their lives, in a glorious city that hardly remembered a time when night walkers moved among them.